I0665276

SWeet CHeeKS

aNd More TaLeS FroM tHe NiCKeL City

by Michael Burns Haggerty

NFB
Buffalo, New York

Copyright © 2016 Michael Burns Haggerty

Printed in the United States of America

Haggerty, Michael Burns

Sweet Cheeks and More Tales from the Nickel City/
Haggerty- 1st Edition

ISBN: 978-0-9984018-5-0

1. Sweet Cheeks and More tales from the Nickel City. 2. Short Stories.
3.Buffalo, New, York. 4. Fiction. 5. Short Fiction.
1. Haggerty.

This is a work of fiction. All characters in this novel are fictitious.
Any resemblance to actual events or locations, unless specified, or
persons, living or dead is entirely coincidental.

No part of this book may be reproduced or transmitted in any form
by any means, electronic or mechanical, including photocopying,
recording, or by any information storage and retrieval system without
permission in writing by the author.

NFB
<<<>>>
No Frills Buffalo/Amelia Press
119 Dorchester Road
Buffalo, New York 14213

For more information visit

nfbpublishing.com

This book is affectionately dedicated, once again, to my Maria

Contents

You never get too high to fall off…nor do you get too low to climb up.

-Tommy McCracken, Chicago Blues Legend

SWeet CHeeKS

S weet Cheeks is sick of me. I can tell by the disgusted look she gives me while I'm bending over tying my work boots and letting my gut, looking like a dull marshmallow, drop over my belt buckle. When she scowls at me like that her face crumples into a rotten apple and her eyes narrow into two evil slits.

Sweet Cheeks sits naked on the bed with her perky little tits and wide hips. She's painting her toes with bright red nail polish called Red Hot Tango, smoking a cigarette, and sipping on her usual coffee sitting on a table next to her, half filled with hot milk, and loaded with about fourteen teaspoons of sugar.

"Have you even considered losing that gut?" she says.

"Come on Sugar, don't start your shit with me now," I say, standing up and throwing on a clean t-shirt. "I got to get to work."

"My ass," Sweet Cheeks says. "You don't work; you run around with your gay buddies bragging about how many women you haven't laid."

"Dammit Sugar, you're mean as hell this morning. You get your ass out and clean carpets all day, see if that ain't work."

"I don't like it when you keep me up all night, Billy. I don't like it at all."

"You didn't have to finish that whole god-dammed bottle, Sweet Cheeks. We would have been just as good with half that," I say.

"You're just a damn fool," Sweet Cheeks says.

I'm moving in on Sweet Cheeks. "Come here," I say, putting her hand on the bulge in my pants. "Hell, I ain't got a gut."

"You're gettin' one and you're gettin' a boner too."

"Then why don't you just lie down and let me fix that," I say, unbuckling my pants and pushing her on the bed.

"Hell, my toenails are still wet," she says, spreading her legs as I plunge into her. She meets me hard and fast and the whole thing is over in about two minutes.

"You sure know how to wake me up, baby," she says, lighting another cigarette.

I pull up my pants, light a Marlboro, and head to work.

*****

Joey B looks rough this morning. I can tell he's pulled another all-nighter. His hair's a mess and his eyes are red and he's got that pissed-off look that tells me he's not going to be good-ol' Joey B for at least an hour or so.

Each crew member meets at George's apartment at 7:00 AM sharp. George owns the business and the office is in his apartment. He's a dead ringer for Harpo Marx. The only difference is his head of curls is sweet-cola black, but his big nose, bulging eyes, and heavy lips are the same as Harpo's. George doesn't put up with being late and if you stroll in after 7 o'clock more than a couple of times you're fired from working for Advanced Carpet Cleaning.

George has three vans and three crews, with two guys on each crew. I've been working with Joey B for the last couple of months. Joey B's a giant Polack with a wide face and big round light blue eyes that protrude from his head giving him the look of some sort of prehistoric fish swimming in the deepest depths of the ocean. Everything about him is thick: his neck, his lips, his fingers, his calves. Joey B plays guitar in a punk-rock band called The Piranhas. He plays with his girlfriend who does the singing. I watched her one night wearing nothing but a garbage bag and combat boots singing a raw, fast, and frantic version of *I Got You Babe*. Joey B sang the Sonny Bono part.

Our routine is the same every morning. George hands us our scheduled jobs attached to a clipboard. The calls have been spread out, allowing us time to get from one job to the next. All of the cleaning jobs should be completed by 6 o'clock. If there are no problems we are pulling into the office right about that time and calling it a day. Sometimes we get in earlier and sometimes, if there are problems, we come in later. After George hands us our jobs we get into our vans and check the equipment and the cleaning supplies. I run the scrubber, a machine with a rotating brush and a tank to hold soapy water and Joey B follows behind with the steamer, a powerful vacuum that sucks in the dirty water. Once the equipment is checked we head to Bertha's Diner and start the morning off with eggs, coffee, and cigarettes. It's always the six of us: me and Joey B, George and a scrawny newcomer named Brown, and Rughead Dan and his partner Rocky Parlotto, two muscular jocks who love drinking, fighting, and cleaning rugs. By 8:30 we are in our vans and on the road. Our first job is always scheduled for 9 o'clock.

I drive and Joey B looks at the map.

"The fucking Falls," he says. "I hate going up to Niagara Falls."

Our first job is easy: Living room, dining room and hallway. It's our special: two rooms and a hallway for $62.00. We even include Scotchgard to help protect the carpets and keep them clean, but that's a dirty little lie. We don't actually *have* Scotchgard, just a jug filled with soapy water. Our next job is a living room, dining room, hallway and three bedrooms. We sell them Scotchgard for the bedrooms at five bucks a room. We knock out a couple of more jobs and are pulling into George's by 5:30.

*****

When I get home I can see that Sweet Cheeks hasn't done much around the place. She is sitting on the sofa with her bare feet stretched before her on the coffee table drinking a vodka and Mountain Dew and watching the local news. She is putting her cigarette out in an over-flowing ashtray. On the table sits a half-eaten turkey sub in a Jim's Steakout wrapper and an opened bag of chips.

"I worked hard today, baby." I say, moving toward her, lifting her head, and giving her a kiss on the mouth. "Move over and let me sit down."

"Damn, you stink. What the hell you have for lunch?" she says.

"I guess I had a little onion on my burger," I say.

"Well, go brush your teeth, then."

"Shut your mouth, baby. I ain't movin' right now,"
I say.

Sweet Cheeks gets up in a huff and I watch her
little ass shuffle toward the kitchen. She returns with an
opened can of Budweiser and hands it to me.

"Here," she says.

"What's to eat around here? I don't smell anything
cooking."

"I haven't had time," she says. "I'll throw something
together."

*****

Sweet Cheeks is a whore. She has a small racket,
a faithful cliental who call her and set up appointments.
She takes them into a spare bedroom all decorated like
an Egyptian whore's tent. It's got a low bed with a draping
canopy made from sheer colorful linens. The room is
perfumed with incense and filled with mirrors, statues,
busts, gold vases and a bunch of big leafed plants. That's
Sweet Cheeks thing, to dress up like one of those chicks
in Arabian Nights and let guys come over and fuck her
for a hundred bucks or so. She only does this on week-
days, the rest of the time she spends with me.

Sweet Cheeks' name is Carol Barnes, but I've never
called her Carol. She doesn't even look like a Carol; it's

too plain a name for her. I met her when I broke my arm falling off a ladder while painting my mother's garage. It was a stupid move, standing on the top rung, stretching to get paint onto the peak. The ladder slid and I fell and busted my arm up good. Before losing her job, Sweet Cheeks worked at the reception desk at The Buffalo General and when I saw her I believed she was the most beautiful women I had ever laid my eyes on. My doctor had a small office in the hospital. I would go there every few weeks until he was satisfied that my arm was healed. I wooed Sweet Cheeks right there at the desk. It took a couple of times, but I finally got her out and we drank a whole bunch of beer down at Ulrich's Tavern, then went to her house and had a fine time.

Later that evening, I watched as she slid a needle into her arm and experienced the relaxing warmth that would calm her down and control our relationship.

*****

This morning we are in the van driving to our first job-a living room, dining room, hallway and bedroom and-Joey B's explaining blackjack to me.

"If you're at the Casino, the easiest game to win is blackjack. Fuck the machines; fuck roulette, they're designed for you to lose, but in blackjack you at least gotta chance, you're only playing against one guy, the dealer. There might be other guys at the table, but you only gotta beat the dealer. If the dealer folds, everyone at the table wins the hand. All you gotta do is get more points than the dealer without going over twenty-one. The cards 2 through 10 have their face value. The Jack, Queen and King are worth 10 points each, and the Ace is worth one or eleven points, your choice. Don't get me wrong, you can lose your shit, but it's about the odds and you got better odds with blackjack than any other game. I've won some cash playing blackjack," Joe B says.

"How much you win?"

"Shit, I won six-hundred bucks one night, right up at the casino," Joey B says. "I keep it simple. If I have less than seventeen points I take a hit; I take another card. If I have seventeen or more I stay. It works out good for me that way. I'm telling you Billy, you want to make some money, go to the casino and play blackjack. Stick to that rule, though; stay slow and steady on the rule of seventeen. Take your time and you'll get what you need. Learn how to do it first and then go on up. I'll bring a deck of cards tomorrow and show you how it's done."

The next morning we are crammed in a booth at Bertha's and I've won a bunch of hands at blackjack. Joey B's the dealer and the rest of us are eating eggs and bacon while he throws cards at us in rapid fire. We're not playing with money, just learning the groove. I play the hit below seventeen and hold at seventeen or above strategy, and have won more than I've lost. Joey B teaches us if you get two starting cards of the same face value, you have the option to split the hand in two. You place another bet of the same size as the original bet and play on with two hands he tells us.

"You can win twice as much that way," Joey B says.

*****

Sweet Cheeks is in a sluggish mood. When I come home from work she's in one of those get ups. She's got on a golden bikini top and all this sheer colorful silk is draping off her. Her belly's showing and she's wearing gold sandals with her feet covered with flowered henna tattoos.

"Can you not look like that when I get home?" I ask.

"I'm lovely," she says and pulls a jewelry box from under the coffee table. From the box she takes out a needle, a spoon, and a baggie filled with a dull white powder. I watch as she carefully prepares her syringe. Sweet Cheeks pulls the syringe back and bright red blood slowly swirls inside the cylinder. She pushes the plunger gently into her vein, loosens the belt, and lightly slips the needle out. Sweet Cheeks falls back into the couch; her eyes are closed, her mouth is open, and a tiny stream of saliva slides down the side of her mouth. I watch her for a moment, then go into the kitchen and take a Budweiser from the refrigerator. I take a long pull from the Bud and let the cold liquid slide down my throat. I tilt the can and empty it and grab another. When I get back into the living room Sweet Cheeks is looking at me through a delicate haze. She *is* lovely, I think to myself.

*****

The next morning Sweet Cheeks is in a pissy mood. She sits cross-legged and naked on the bed taking cotton balls doused in nail polish remover and cleaning the Red Hot Tango from her toes. Her coffee and cigarette are in place. Her skin is delicate and pale and I see the red needle marks climbing up her arm like a sad case of measles. I am putting on my work boots and looking for a clean shirt.

"How long are you going to clean those damn rugs?" Sweet Cheeks asks.

"What do you mean, Sugar?"

"When are you gonna stop pussy-footin' around and get yourself a job that makes some money? I'm getting tired living like this, Billy. You've got to take better care of me."

"Baby, I might know a way I can make some good money," I say.

"Let me hear it, baby."

"Blackjack," I say.

"Blackjack?"

"Yep, blackjack. It's a good way to make money at the casino. Joey B says, over time, it's a sure thing."

"Joey B's an idiot," Sweet Cheeks says. "Why are you listening to an idiot, Billy?"

"We've been playing every day at breakfast," I say. "I win much more than I lose."

"What are you winning, baby?"

"Well, I'm not winning *anything*, but I'm learning the *skill*. You could say I'm in training and when I get some money I'm going straight up to the Casino and I'm going to win big for us, Sweet Cheeks."

"Baby, you're a damn fool," Sweet Cheeks says. "When you get money? Boy, I'd sure like to see that."

"Baby, I'm not a fool. I promised I was going to get you out of this mess here and we would live in Costa Rica, right on the Pacific Ocean where it hardly costs anything to live and we are going to swim in the blue sea and eat all the seafood we can and drink ice cold beers for everyday of our lives."

Sweet Cheeks lies down and pulls me onto her naked body. "You're a dreamer, baby; I like that," she says.

*****

"Guess how I won four hundred bucks last night?" Joey B says.

"Blackjack?" I say.

"Goddamn right," Joey B. says. "I was only up there for about an hour and once I got in the groove, I started hitting. Rule of seventeen, brother. It was fucking magic!"

Joey B's countenance is a mixture of contentment and pride. We are in the van driving on LeBrun Avenue. Joey B's sitting in his seat leaning back with the clipboard on his lap and his arm out the window. The streets have widened and curve through bucolic landscapes, the lawns are large and meticulously manicured, managed by a variety of landscaping services with shirtless workers riding stand-up power mowers. Each home has its own extensive garden with colorful winding flower paths, rambling vines, and blooming shrubs. The homes are big stone structures, large and magnificent. SUV's, BMWs and Mercedes Benzes sit sparkling under the hot sun in wide driveways.

"This sure beats my neighborhood," Joey B says.

"Hell, if I lived out here I wouldn't have one of those Beamers or SUV's, I'd have me a fuckin' white and cherry-red, mint '57 Chevy sittin' in my driveway."

"That's a badass car," I say.

"Sure fuckin' is," Joey B says.

We are pulling into the driveway of an enormous English Tudor style home. Joey B reads the clipboard, "Living room, dining room, family room, three bedrooms and two hallways; this will take us a couple of hours," he says.

At the door, a slender older woman casually dressed in brown penny loafers, slim bright green pants, and a white polo shirt greets us. Her eye-glasses are nestled on top of her head in overly-teased golden hair, and pink lipstick covers a wrinkled mouth. Her face is crumpled and deeply tanned and her eyes are bright blue. She wears the countenance of having money, spending winters in Florida, holidays on the Cape, an annual European trip, and summers on the golf course at the country club. She eyes us with vague disdain, leads us into her living room, and tells us to be careful lugging in our equipment. Joey B gives her the finger when she's looking in my direction.

The carpets before us hardly need a cleaning; no soil marks or stains anywhere. It is as if this woman is spending money for the sake of spending. Maybe a carpet cleaning truck parked in her driveway elevates her status in front of the neighbors. I don't really know, but I'm thankful for the easy job.

It is quiet in the house and the woman has left us alone. We clean the living room, dining room, and family room, and then carry the equipment upstairs toward the bedrooms. Inside the master bedroom the walls, carpet, and furniture all blend into a soft cream colored milieu. The woman is lying on the bed with her shoes kicked off and laying on the floor beside the bed. Her toenails are painted the same shade of pink as her lipstick. Bunions protrude from the joints of her big toes and a fly walks aimlessly about her forehead. Joey B knocks at the door and the lady gives no response.

"We're here to clean the bedroom," he says.

We watch her and realize she is not moving.

"What the Christ?" Joey B says.

"Well, isn't that something," I say. "Do you think she's dead?"

"Hey!" Joey B says. "You hear us, or what?"

We move toward the bed and I shake her shoulder to wake her. Nothing. Her glasses are tilted crookedly on the bridge of her nose and a copy of *Revolutionary Road* by Richard Yates is resting on her chest.

"Christ, the old broad kicked the bucket reading a book," Joey B says.

"She sure did," I say. "We better call George and we should call the police too."

"Yes, we better call, but let's just wait a couple of minutes and think about this," Joey B says.

"Think about what?"

"Maybe she's got something we might want."

"Like what?"

"This old broad's loaded," Joey B says. "She's gotta have some cash around here somewhere."

"I don't know about that," I say. "I don't want to get involved in anything crazy."

"There's nothing to get involved in. If she's got some cash, we take it; no one will know. We'll call the cops and let George know and they'll be glad we were here when she kicked. They'll be thankful she didn't lie here dead for too long. It doesn't look like a robbery, nothin's busted up. Hell, we're not intruders, she's the one who hired *us*; we'll come out looking like heroes."

This is a fact. The woman is certainly dead. Joey B figures everything is on schedule and if we were going to help ourselves, now is our window of opportunity. If we wait too long, then, well, suspicion could arise.

Joey B rummages through dresser drawers and I

enter a huge walk-in closet loaded with racks of shoes and crisp color coded dresses hanging around the perimeter of the closet. Along the walls, on shelves, sit stacks of folded pants and there are a couple revolving racks loaded with belts of every shade and color. On the shelf under a pile of pants is a metal box and in the box are bank envelopes filled with crisp, new one hundred dollar bills. I bring the box out and place it on the bed for Joey B to look at.

"Bingo," he says and begins counting the envelopes. "Hell, there're twenty envelopes with a thousand dollars in each one. That's twenty-thousand dollars, Billy boy!

"I don't know; I don't want any trouble," I say.

"I'm telling you, this old broad's loaded. She's got more money in the bank then we'll ever see in our lives. This is *just in case money* for her, a little stash. No one is going to know. Nobody could prove we took any money. I'll put it behind the back panel in the van and we'll call George and the police and report this thing. This is clean, Billy. I'm telling you."

*****

Joey B is nursing a rum and coke and I am drinking a whiskey and ginger. Three disheveled Japanese looking businessmen drinking long neck Budweiser's and chain smoking Marlboros share the blackjack table with us. Their suits are rumpled and their neckties hang crookedly under open collars. The dealer is dark skinned with a soft face and shoeshine-black hair. I peg him to be from India. He is wearing black pants, a white shirt, and black tie and he is losing to the table. A pit boss arrives and watches the action carefully and after a few more hands decides to change dealers. Joey B and I collect our chips and move to another table. This time the dealer is a slight, bald man hosting a couple of fat guys wearing Buffalo Bills Jerseys losing their shit one hand at a time. Joey B and I stick to our rule of seventeen and slowly build our winnings.

The *Seneca Niagara Casino* is a cacophony of lights, bells, sirens, and buzzers. Slot machines whizz and whirl and the dank scent of cigarette smoke permeates the air. Joey B has explained our strategy and we are sticking to it. He told me: "We are not telling anybody about the money, not even our girlfriends. We're gonna go to all the casinos around here, Seneca Niagara, Casino Niagara, Buffalo Creek, Hamburg Gaming, and we're gonna slowly build on our winnings. We don't want to draw any attention. Then, we're going to the Fallsview Casino and get ourselves onto one of those *high limit* tables where we can make some real money. From there we're golden and we're gonna have a nice little chunk of change stashed."

*****

It's been a month since we helped ourselves to the old lady's loot. We are still cleaning carpets as if nothing's changed. Not a word has been said about the old lady's money. Sweet Cheeks is still whoring and shooting dope and giving me shit about making a better life for her. I tell her more about Costa Rica, sandy beaches, tall palm trees, and she calls me a dreamer, but little does she know, I'm gonna make a good life for her. She'll be pleasantly surprised when I lay it all on her. Joey B and I have our secret hiding places where we are stashing our winnings. We have around twenty-five G's apiece.

*****

Joey B and I pull the van into the office after a long tiresome week. It is Friday and the thought of a couple days off from cleaning carpets is welcoming.

"Jesus," he says. "I'm getting tired of this shit, working my ass off. You ready, Billy? You ready to go up to Fallsview and get on some of those *high limit* tables? Our luck is good lately. We can make some real changes if we hit."

"I feel good," I say.

"Put on a nice shirt and pants; we don't want to go in there looking like a couple of bums. I'll pick you up at eight o'clock."

When I get home Sweet Cheeks is sitting on the sofa pressing towel filled with ice against her mouth. She is in her Egyptian get-up. Her hair is a mess and her face is red and swollen. Her lip is split and the blood from her mouth has stained the towel crimson-red.

"What the hell?" I say.

"He was a referral from a regular client. I didn't know him. He got rough and started slapping the shit out of me. I told him I don't play rough and he just got angrier and angrier."

In a strange way Sweet Cheeks looks comically pitiful with her red face, watery eyes, and black eyeshadow running in rivulets down her cheeks.

"Get out of those clothes and take a warm bath," I say to her and then I tell her the whole story. I tell her about learning how to play blackjack like a pro. I tell her about the dead woman and the money and how I've bumped up my share to twenty-five G's, and I tell her Joey B's picking me up and we're heading to Fallsview where we can really make some cash. "Who knows, if we win big tonight maybe real soon we can get on a bus and head to Vegas and make enough money to get to Costa

Rica. My luck's good, baby, I feel real good."

I show Sweet Cheeks the cash and her eyes brighten and she says, "Holy Shit, Billy, you're not kiddin'!"

*****

We enter a private salon and sit at one of those high stakes tables. This is where the serious gamblers come. It is much quieter here than in the main casino. Hardly any words are spoken; we listen only to the dry shuffle and snap of crisp, shiny cards being dealt towards us. We are at a table with two men in tailored suits and meticulously cut hair. Joey B and I look out of place, but we are sticking to the rule of seventeen and we are up ten-thousand on a hundred dollar a bet table. We have our own server standing behind us and he is delivering us two fingers of bourbon on ice. We sip the bourbon slowly and concentrate on the cards, the dealer, and the pit boss carefully eyeing us.

We are now up twelve thousand apiece and the table has turned the dealer's way. The men in suits have lost close to three thousand and we have lost fifteen hundred in a matter of only a few hands. Joey B is thinking; he is doing the math in his head. He turns to me and nods that it is time to leave. We walk from the dimly lit silent room and enter the loud, echoing main casino.

"Our luck turned," Joey B says. "A calm man knows when his luck's run out, at least for now. A lot of people would have stayed and got wiped out. We made it outta here ten G's richer, though. It's Vegas now, buddy."

I am excited about the cash. Ten crisp one hundred dollar bills and a fifty dollar bill fits securely in my front pocket. Sweet Cheeks is going to be happy as hell. I imagine her sitting on our veranda in Costa Rica, looking calmly over the glittering ocean, sipping a cold gin and tonic. Her legs are stretched before her, tanned and lovely.

Joey B drops me off in front of our place. He nods in my direction and shakes my hand.

"I'll see you Monday morning," he says.

"Okay, you have a good weekend," I say.

Inside, the apartment is dark except for the soft flickering light from the television playing one of those infomercials about some sort of juice machine. Muscled men in tight shirts and shorts, and bikini clad women happily smile at one another while cramming all kinds of fruits and vegetables into a blender and marvel at their magical concoctions. I figure Sweet Cheeks has gone to sleep, so I go into the kitchen, make a ham sandwich, pop open a Budweiser, and sit at the kitchen table skimming through the *Buffalo News*. Afterwards, I put the sandwich stuff away, toss the can into the recycle bin, and head into the bathroom to brush my teeth. I flick on the light and Sweet Cheeks is lying naked in the tub with a sheer pink scarf hanging loosely around her bicep and a needle floating at her feet. Burned out candles surround the perimeter of the bathtub. Sweet Cheeks is very pale and I place my hand on her cold shoulder.

"Why couldn't you wait for me, Sweet Cheeks?" I say to her. "I told you I was going to get us out of here."

I sit on the toilet holding Sweet Cheek's hand in mine and I let her know how beautiful she is. We sit that way for quite a while until I pull her from the tub and carry her to her Egyptian room and lay her on the bed. I pat dry Sweet Cheeks with a soft towel and dress her in sheer silks and place the gold sandals on her feet. I am momentarily at a loss as to what to do. I don't know her family; we never talked about them, but I'm sure there must be someone who will claim her.

Before I head out the door, I write a short note and leave it on the table next to where Sweet Cheeks lies. It reads: *I am sorry for what I've done. I almost made it out of here. Yours truly, Carol Barnes.*

*****

The woman at the Greyhound ticket counter looks

into her computer screen and lets me know bus fare to Las Vegas is two hundred and twenty-nine dollars and it will take two days, five hours and fifty minutes. That seems like a real long time, but I've got nothing better to do. I give her cash for a ticket, board the bus, and move toward the back row. The bus is about half full. After a while the driver turns on the engine and we pull out of the Ellicott Street Station and head through the quiet empty city streets. The seats are comfortable and I adjust mine back and get absorbed in the steady hum of the Greyhound's engine. I look out the window and watch as the lights fade from Buffalo and we drive silently on the highway pushing into the black emptiness. I am thinking that I will call the police in the morning, and I am thinking of Joey B and the slow and steady rule of seventeen.

Sweet Cheeks originally published in *Scintilla*

Love, Honor, and Obey

I t began with a shotgun wedding. Jenny insisted she walk down the aisle. She wanted a priest's blessing for this one.

"I am walking that aisle, Donnie. It doesn't matter how things are, I'm walking down that aisle," she said.

Jenny strolled down the tiny church's aisle in a pure white Chantilly lace wedding dress and a seven-month baby bump leading the way. We went through the whole ritual promising to love, honor, and obey…all witnessed by our closest friends and family. The marriage was abruptly finished a little over half a year later. The love, honor, and obey stuff hardly lasted.

*****

I met Jenny in June at the end of our senior year in high school through my best buddy Greg, a guy I'd been hanging with since kindergarten. His girlfriend Maryjane was a tough boyish-chick with kinky hair and a chipmunk face. She didn't like me much. She was sick and tired of me tagging along with them. She needed to hook me up with someone and figured her friend Jenny might do the trick. Maryjane set the whole thing up.

I lived in a small two bedroom apartment on Parkside Avenue with my dad at the time. He and my mother split a year earlier and the old man was always out late into the night or staying over at one of his girlfriend's places. Maryjane figured it wouldn't be a problem to invite them over, have a few beers, and listen to some music.

It was on a Friday, in the early evening, when they came over. Greg carried a big box of pepperoni pizza in both hands and Maryjane held a twelve pack of Labatt's Blue beer. When Jenny entered, I realized I had seen her in the hallways in school. She moved gracefully, had a delicate round face, and a very short reddish-brown bob-haircut. Her eyes were shadowy, green, and serious. She stayed rather quiet all evening. Maryjane popped open four beers and Greg opened the pizza box on the coffee table in the living room. The room filled with the yeasty scent of fresh dough and mozzarella cheese. Puddles of grease lay in concave slices of pepperoni. I threw a cd into the stereo and we listened to Pink Floyd's *Wish You Were Here.*

*****

Sparks flew and we liked each other right away. I saw her the next day and the day after that. We started off like any other excited couple, inseparable, both of us infatuated with whatever the other said or did. About a week into it, we lay in my bed discovering the sensual pleasures of long quiet afternoons. Lying close to one another under the weight of a feathered comforter, we made plans to build a future. Jenny was going to be a nurse. I was thinking about becoming a journalist. We both graduated from our high school at the end of June and had the whole summer to spend with one another.

We managed to spend time together every day. I had a job working during the week as a landscaper with two fat cousins named Dick and Dave. Both had massive necks, square heads, deep-brown beady eyes and reddish-pink complexions. Both were in full blown sweat mode by 9:00 AM. I figured Dave might be what you could have labeled mildly retarded. I mostly weeded and raked and picked up after them. They never let me use the big mower. That was a prize for the most experienced crew members. These boys moved at a frantic pace. They were determined to get the jobs done quickly and get out of work before that hot afternoon sun became too stifling.

In the late afternoons Jenny and I spent our time in my blue Plymouth Horizon crisscrossing Western New York, swimming at beaches along the sandy shores of Lake Erie, hiking the deep-wooded trails of Zoar Valley, or fishing for perch at the mouth of Eighteen Mile Creek. Jenny kept a Coleman cooler iced with cold beers, fried chicken, and potato salad. We happily ambled through the long, hot summer.

When September came, both of us were focused and energized and enrolled as freshman in college. Jenny attended a small private college to get her nursing degree and I was enrolled at Buffalo State College and accepted into their Journalism program. The landscaping job ended and, for a few extra bucks, I waited tables in the evenings at an upscale restaurant on Delaware Avenue called Oliver's.

We were what you would call *a couple* and had devoted ourselves to one another. We scheduled our classes in order to spend mornings or afternoons with one another and we spent every weekend together. Seasons changed from cold to hot, dark to light, wet to dry as is the nature of things. Jenny became the intimate being that ignited the very purpose of my existence. Life was good. Except for the occasional cramming for finals or the endless readings and projects college requires, we got through it all pretty well.

We graduated four years later and moved in together, finding a flat on Anderson Place, a quiet tree-lined street off of Elmwood Avenue. The apartment was large and bright with hardwood floors, high ceilings, and ornate wooden door frames. A red-brick fireplace and leaded glass book cases filled the living room. Jenny worked as a nurse at Children's Hospital a few streets down from our place. I worked in the promotions department at WNED TV trying to break into a writing job for the Buffalo News. I hung onto my restaurant job a couple nights a week and things were going pretty well. We were living comfortably. Everything we needed we had.

Over time my responsibilities increased at the television station. I was doing more writing. A few of my pieces got noticed by the Buffalo News and I received a call from an editor offering me a job writing local news features. I received a nice bump in my salary allowing me to quit the job at Oliver's. Jenny and I shared our evenings and weekends enjoying the closeness and solitude we were able to manage when we first met.

*****

Sometimes everything in life just works out. It

runs perfectly like a cold, clear mountain stream flowing over glass smooth stones. Management at the hospital recognized Jenny's talents. Before long she was promoted as head nurse in the emergency room. They boosted her salary; between the two of us, we were pulling in a pretty good buck. Jenny suggested we move out of our apartment and get ourselves into a condo. As our lucky star glowed brilliantly, it just so happened that Jenny's Aunt Irene was being moved from her apartment to live out the rest of her years at an upscale nursing home. Aunt Irene had a lot of money and not much family and none of them wanted to live in an apartment building in downtown Buffalo. They were all comfortably settled right where they were, but Jenny *did* want to live close to downtown and she fell in love with Aunt Irene's eighth-floor beauty at the Campanile on Delaware Avenue. It was arranged that we would buy it from her and take out a mortgage. The Campanile rose from the corner of Delaware and Bryant streets in elegant-urbane-grandeur. From our living-room window we could see the wide-tree-lined avenue heading toward downtown. Mansions from a bygone era stood in magnificent splendor along the way. The Campanile with its Corinthian columns and terra cotta ornamentation, surrounding the windows, was a place I never figured I'd be living in.

"Just give me a chance to decorate this place," Jenny said. "I'll make this a wonderfully cozy home for us."

And she did. The place was perfect and our lives were perfect.

*****

One afternoon, after work, I got off the elevator and opened the door to our apartment. Jenny looked at me with those serious green eyes and announced she was pregnant. I could not read her expression. She showed no sign of happiness or displeasure, her countenance was matter of fact.

"Is this good?" I asked.

"Yes, it's good," she said. "I'm just surprised. I didn't realize. I didn't know. I took a home test and it read positive."

"Well then, this is great news," I said, moving toward her and placing my arms around her waist giving her a tight hug.

"I made an appointment with my doctor and I'm scheduled see him on Thursday," Jenny said, pulling away. "We will know more from there."

*****

Thursday came. I took the morning off and went

to the Doctor's with Jenny. Doctor Gugino had a bright office with a bubbly receptionist who took Jenny's information and motioned for us to take a seat in the waiting room until the doctor was ready to see us. Jenny was calm and excited and said she hoped we would have a little girl, but, of course, a boy would be just as fine. She tossed out names: Lily, Alice, Ellie, Claire, and asked which I liked best.

"I like them all," I said. "They're good names. You pick."

"Claire is a good name. I could see us having a little girl and naming her Claire. It's a good name and you can't shorten it."

"I like it too," I said.

"Now, for a boy: Jack, Henry, Oliver – what do you think?"

"Henry has a nice sound. You don't see too many Henry's around anymore. I think it's a fine name."

"I think it's a fine name too," she said. "Claire or Henry; I like those names. They're both strong names. I could live with Claire or Henry."

"It's settled then," I said.

"Yes," Jenny said. "It's settled."

*****

A few months later we got married and the wedding was quiet and quaint, just the way Jenny wanted it. I had never seen anyone as beautiful as Jenny walking toward me down the aisle, her shy smile capturing my heart at that very moment.

Jenny was able to work right up to the time she delivered. Her paychecks continued to come rolling in. I was getting a lot of lead stories. One was about a killer who threw a baby over the Grand Island Bridge while in the grip of a schizophrenic episode. That story got national attention on the wires giving me quite a bit of exposure.

It was decided that Jenny would deliver the baby at Children's Hospital. Doctor Gugino was well respected at the hospital and Jenny was comfortable with him.

On the day of her delivery we were at the Albright-Knox Art Gallery looking at a collection of works by Jackson Pollack. We were looking at a piece titled *Convergence* when her water broke running down her leg and puddling onto the museum floor.

"I think it's time," she said.

"Let's go," I said.

*****

The delivery room was brightly lit with florescent lights. We were placed with a large black woman who introduced herself as Ida. Ida wore a blue smock and a kind smile.

"I'm gonna be your labor nurse," she told Jenny. "You might say I'm your best friend right now."

Ida gently covered Jenny with a blue blanket, propped a pillow behind her head, and guided her legs into a set of stirrups. Jenny let out high-pitched screams as her contractions became more intense. Her cheeks were flush and beads of perspiration hung on her upper lip. Ida wiped her face with a cool, damp towel.

"You're doing fine, girl," she said.

Doctor Gugino entered the room and looked under the blanket into Jenny's spread legs.

"You're doing great," he said. "You're at ten centimeters."

"It hurts, Doctor," Jenny said. "It hurts real bad!"

"You doin' okay, honey," Ida said.

"I want you to push," Doctor Gugino said. "Push real hard."

"I can't!" Jenny screamed.

"Get that baby outta there. Give it a good push with all your might." Ida said.

Jenny sucked in a deep breath and exhaled while pushing. Veins protruded from her forehead and tears welled in her eyes.

"Push, girl. Push harder," Ida said.

"I can't," Jenny cried. "I can't. It's too fucking painful!"

"I can see the head, Jenny," Doctor Gugino said. "Once more with everything you've got."

Jenny pushed her shoulders forward grinding her chin onto her chest letting out a low-pitch-guttural growl through clenched teeth. Ida cradled the back of her neck firmly telling her to push that baby right into this world. I moved around to get a closer look watching the baby glide out of Jenny's spread legs. The baby slid into the bright room looking like a slimy creature from another planet. It spun its head and screamed in our direction. Doctor Gugino announced that it was a girl. Ida took the baby from Doctor Gugino rubbing the gooey paste off of her. She suctioned the baby's nose and throat, gave her a quick injection of vitamin K, and rubbed ointment over her eyes. Ida wrapped the baby in a soft blanket while Doctor Gugino pulled Jenny's placenta out to one more tiresome scream.

"Well, here you go little mama," Ida said, placing the bundled baby into Jenny's arms.

*****

At three months Claire had all of the signs of a healthy baby. Her skin was rosy-pink, her legs pudgy, and her hair was fine and delicate as silken corn threads. She slept soundly and when she woke in the middle of the night, Jenny lifted her out of her crib and brought her into bed to feed. In the stillness of the night, Claire sucked her mother's nipple quietly without fussing.

Jenny enjoyed being on maternity leave and the hospital was good about giving her all of the time off she needed.

"I need to have Claire a year...a year before I even consider taking her to a day-care. I love her so much; she's such a good baby. The first year is so important to be with her mother. I just don't think I can give her up," Jenny said.

"That's no problem with me," I said. "I love the fact you're able to stay home with her."

*****

I was standing next to a taxi on a broken-glass littered parking lot on the East side of Buffalo. The cops had previously taken the cabdriver from his car. His throat was slit from ear to ear. Blood splattered the inside of the windshield, the dashboard, and pooled in the driver seat. The cabbie was dead. Whoever took him out was gone without a trace. Cops in their squad cars formed a perimeter around the cab. An irritated detective in a white shirt stretched over a large gut scoured the scene looking for clues. I tried to get information from him. All he could tell me was he had a dead cabbie and some fucker slit his throat in broad daylight. "For a god-dammed fare," he figured. It was at that time Jenny called me, in a panic, telling me Claire had fallen from her high chair hitting her head on the kitchen table.

"Dammit, I didn't strap her in," she sobbed. "Please come home!"

When I arrived, Jenny had Claire in her arms pressing an ice-pack firmly to her forehead. She looked okay to me.

"She just slid from her chair. I didn't have her secure. I've failed at my most fundamental duty, keeping Claire safe."

I looked at the baby. She wriggled contently in her mother's arms.

"Here, let me see," I said examining a small red bump on her forehead. Her eyes were clear and she wore a content look. "She looks okay, she's smiling. Babies are resilient, they can take a fall; she's okay."

"Do you think so?"

"Of course," I said. She's fine."

*****

Jenny became more and more agitated. She doubted her motherly instincts. "I need to protect Claire. She could be in danger. I'm not doing a good job. She doesn't smile much since she fell from her high-chair. I hope she's okay."

"She's perfectly fine and she smiles a lot. I see her smiling all of the time."

"You don't understand. Head trauma can be complicated," Jenny said. "It can be very complicated. I read just one fall can result in a concussion or seizures or even autism. I may have harmed her for life."

"You need to stop reading that stuff. It's making you crazy. Claire's fine and we both know it."

"If you cared for her you wouldn't be so quick to diagnose," she said.

"Diagnose? She's fine; make an appointment with Doctor Gugino if that will make you feel better."

Jenny gave me a long faraway look. She looked at Claire, lowered her head and cried. A little later she dialed Doctor Gugino's office for an appointment.

*****

"Babies have built in systems that absorb falls," Doctor Gugino said. "Nature keeps them pliable. A baby's bones and skull are resilient enough to absorb repeated falls; they absorb falls better than you or me. It's all perfectly natural."

"I hope so," Jenny said. "I couldn't live with myself if I ever hurt her."

"Of course," Doctor Gugino said. "You're a typical new mother. Babies are tougher than you think."

"My baby doesn't smile anymore. I haven't seen her smile since she fell. Why, Doctor Gugino, why is that?"

"You're a Nurse, Jenny." Doctor Gugino said. "Take your emotion out of this and think like a medical person. Everything is perfectly fine."

"I see Claire smile a lot," I added. "You're letting your imagination get the best of you."

"That's bullshit!" Jenny snapped abruptly picking up Claire and heading toward the door. "I know my child and she's not happy. She's fucking angry with me."

Doctor Gugino gave me a pensive look.

"We'll talk later," he said. "These behaviors can be common for new mothers. Keep an eye on her for now."

*****

A few weeks later Jenny invited her sister Andrea and husband John over for dinner.

"I haven't seen my sister in forever," she said. "Will you cook for us?"

"Of course; I'd love to," I said, thinking this was the first time I'd seen her happily looking forward to something in a long time. I figured I could handle an evening with the two of them.

John got caught up buying and selling corporate real-estate and was making more money than he would ever know what to do with. Andrea was an attorney, but had been spending most of her time coordinating cultural events and running social events at the Twentieth Century Club. She enjoyed the status of an up and coming socialite. She tackled some legal work, mainly real-estate transactions through her husband's company. Together they were both doing A-Okay.

They arrived at our apartment right on time. John greeted us both a warm hug. He patted me on the back and handed over a bottle of Chateau Lafite telling me to save *this beauty* for a special occasion. Andrea removed her coat, handed it to me, and scanned the apartment.

"It's absolutely fabulous!" she said, looking at her husband. "John, why don't we live in the city? It's so much more elegant; I could leave the 'burbs in a heartbeat."

"With a place like this, I believe I could too," he answered.

Andrea displayed an extraordinary resemblance to her sister. She wore the same serious expression and moved in the same delicate fashion. John was tall and handsome with a healthy crop of raven-black hair. His eyebrows were thick and his eyes were dark. He had the look of a model or perhaps one of those good looking leading men from the films in the forties. Together they were a handsome sight.

"I smell something incredible," he said, lifting his nose with a glowing smile. "What have you cooked up this time?"

"I made veal scaloppini with brown butter and capers over angel-hair pasta."

"You are too much!" John said. "I'm lucky if I can put together a sandwich."

"That's a fact," Andrea said. "Where is that precious baby?"

"Come with me, Andrea," Jenny said, taking her hand. "Claire's sleeping in her room. We can check on her."

"That's our cue, John," I said. "Let's make some drinks. Martinis for the ladies?"

"Yum," Andrea said. "Make mine extra dirty!"

"Me too," said Jenny.

"How about you, John? Will you have a Martini?

"If it's all the same to you, if you have some rye, I'd love an old-fashioned."

"How's Rittenhouse Rye?"

"Perfect," John said.

A few moments later I had finished the drinks and the girls came back in. I handed them each a martini with three olives.

Andrea looked at her husband, "John, the baby is absolutely adorable. She's precious."

"I'll bet," John said.

"We're not too sure how she is," Jenny said. "She's taken a few falls. They've been my fault. I've been neglectful and I fear she may have some permanent damage. Possibly brain damage. Sometimes, I can't bear to look at her."

"Nonsense," Andrea said. "She's absolutely perfect."

"Well, I feel pretty dangerous being around Claire. I'd rather kill myself than hurt her," Jenny said.

"For heaven's sake," Andrea said giving Jenny a firm look. "Don't talk such nonsense."

"Why don't we sit down in the living room," I said. "I have some appetizers already laid out."

"Wonderful," John said. "By the way, this old-fashioned is perfect."

"My Martini is fabulous," Andrea said. "What kind of gin do you use?"

"Boodles London Dry," I said. "It's classic."

"I'll say," Andrea said. "Look at this incredible spread…yummy…smoked salmon and almonds and olives! You are too much, Donnie."

We ate the appetizers and sipped our drinks. Jenny drank hers quickly and asked for another.

"If you'd like, but we *are* having wine with dinner." I said.

"I think I can handle it, Donnie," she said vacantly.

Jenny drank another and kicked her shoes off. Her ears reddened and her eyes became glassy. We ate the appetizers, finished our drinks, and moved into the dining room where Jenny had set the table with our best china, silverware, and wine glasses. A small bouquet of wild flowers was placed on the center of the table.

"The table is beautiful, Jenny," Andrea said. "Is this Grandmother's china?"

"Yes," Jenny said. "I just love it. I'm so glad to have it."

"I should say," Andrea said. "I received her pearls and you got her good china. I think you got the best of that deal, Sister."

I opened a bottle of pinot noir, poured everyone a glass, excused myself, went in the kitchen and plated the veal. When I returned Jenny's head was lowered. She was crying and Andrea was standing above her with her arms around her shoulders consoling uncontrollable sobs.

"What is this?" I asked.

"Jenny's upset," John said. "Thinks the baby may have cerebral palsy…says she's been giving the child the Landau reflex test and the baby does not always respond."

"For Christ Sakes, there is nothing wrong with our baby," I said.

"There is too something wrong and she's going to suffer all of her life and it's my fault!"

"Oh, honey…you had too much to drink and you need to get some rest. Let me take you in the other room so you can lie down," Andrea said.

Andrea took Jenny into the other room and John pointed a furrowed brow in my direction.

"You have a problem, Donnie. You need to get this taken care of," he said.

*****

Doctor Rachel Feinstein listened with benevolent interest as Jenny confided in her, sharing her concerns.

At the end of the session, Doctor Feinstein scheduled an appointment for three days later and prescribed Zoloft to help Jenny manage her stress. The sessions went on like this, every three days, for about a month. Jenny began to feel the calming effects of the medication. I noticed she was happier and more at ease. Her eyes softened. It seemed that her conversations with Doctor Feinstein lessened her anxiety, eased her away from the harsh irritability that she had so easily clung onto.

*****

It was early January and the hustle of the holidays had come and gone. On this frozen dark morning a low-hanging, slow-moving, lake-effect snow storm pummeled the city, dropping foot after foot of heavy white snow onto the awakening neighborhoods. Cars were parked single file; neighborhoods of white glistening mounds under big snow-laden elms gave each street a tunneled depth of perception. The city stood still. For the remainder of the day the city of Buffalo knelt in defiant stillness while the thrashing continued. By evening a muted unmoving calmness held the city captivated under a deep black sky.

Jenny sat comfortably in a chair quietly looking out from the frosted windowpane to the street below. Claire nestled herself at her bosom and the two of them seemed lost in some inter-connected dream.

"It's so pretty outside," Jenny said. "Let's bundle up and take a walk."

"Sure, that sounds like fun," I said.

We moved quietly down the snowy, silent street. The glacial air held motionless, and the sky was deep blue-black. Enormous plows had burrowed through the streets creating monstrous white embankments illuminated under tall black street lamps. Neighbors tiredly shoveled big chunks of heavy snow piled at the ends of their driveways left haphazardly by the hurried plows. They shoveled sidewalks and pathways that worked up to the front entrances of their homes. A mutual silent understanding pervaded the neighborhoods after a harsh storm, an understanding of survival.

Jenny had Claire firmly snuggled in her carrier. The carrier was strapped to Jenny's chest. Claire was bundled. All that could be seen of her were tiny sparkling eyes looking curiously at the massive piles of fallen snow.

"I feel good, Donnie," Jenny said. "It's peaceful out here, so quiet and beautiful. The snow softens our neighborhood."

"It does," I said.

"It's not always like this, you know."

"I know that."

"I love this baby-carrier," Jenny said. "Claire is so close and protected in here."

"She looks very comfortable," I said.

"I love you, Donnie," Jenny said.

"I love you too," I said.

*****

The storm circled back the next morning dumping more snow on an already beaten city. Buffalo hunkered quietly and patiently, waiting for the chance to dig out once again. The city was shut down. Scrolling texts on local television stations shared an endless list of school and business closings. The Mayor placed a driving ban within the city limits. Only emergency vehicles were allowed on city streets. Outside our apartment, the wind blew furiously. Snow swirled with such a force that nothing could be seen from our window. It was as if we were in the center of an infinite abyss. This continued until late afternoon.

My phone rang. It was the city editor. He wanted an eye-witness story.

"You're close to downtown," he said. "Take a walk, look around, and send me over something right away. I need a fresh update for the Website and the early morning edition."

I hung up the phone and started to get dressed. Jenny sat on the sofa reading. Claire slept soundly at her side.

"I have to take a walk, Jenny. The boss needs a neighborhood story. I'll try to walk to Chippewa Street, see what's going on out there. See if anything's open or moving."

"Bundle up and be careful," she said, lifting her face toward me to kiss it.

"I will," I said, heading out the door, into the elevator, and out the massive doors of the Campanile.

I hiked slowly down Delaware Avenue to Allen Street turning right toward Elmwood Avenue. I had to walk in the street as the sidewalks had long disappeared under the mounting snow. There was no sun and the sky tinged silver-gray. Most of the stores, restaurants and bars were closed. There was no traffic on the usually busy streets. I watched a bundled-up figure tear down the center of Allen Street on a snow mobile. He had a shovel strapped to the back of it. At the corner of Allen and Elmwood the Towne Restaurant was open. The windows were frozen and I could see shadows sitting at booths presumably eating souvlaki's and sipping hot coffee. Across the street at Cantina Loco a tattooed bartender served drinks to those in the neighborhood who could walk from their houses and apartments to wait out the storm while eating big plates of nachos, drinking beer, and throwing back shots of tequila. I moved down Elmwood past the firehouse and toward Chippewa Street. A hidden sun was setting somewhere behind leaden skies, and a false twilight strained to lighten the approaching dusk with one last pathetic silver-tinged sky. As I wandered down the darkened street past more closed restaurants and bars, a bluish-purple sky emerged. The city would sleep early tonight.

At the Campanile Jenny stood quietly looking out the window with Claire strapped securely in her carrier. She opened the window, sending an icy chill swirling into the apartment, and sat on the ledge with her back toward the dark, brittle evening. She leaned backward into the frigid night. While plummeting to the snow-packed sidewalk below, Jenny noticed the leafless tree branches above her extending themselves like a mockingly twisted forest.

I turned left and strolled up Franklin Street watching chimney smoke climbing from grandiose brick homes. I gazed past sheer curtains into open living rooms and dining rooms lit in soft lighting. I looked at paintings adorning the walls, portraits and pastoral scenes hanging in the glow of the big comfortable rooms.

In the distance, I heard the sound of a low rumbling thunder as if it was a guttural growl spat from the Heavens themselves.

PitiFUL OLd MaN

I t was one of those dark, cold damp nights in early November. The wind blew drearily and a swollen sky held somber gray. It had been raining for days and the leaves had fallen from giant trees turning the long, twisting branches bare and brittle. We were in Hyde Park, NY gearing up for my sister's graduation from the Culinary Institute of America. The next morning she would walk the stage, say farewell to her pals, and head into the hot and gritty world of restaurant kitchens armed with a chef's knife and all the cooking knowledge the school had to offer. It was going to be a big day for her and the family had driven from Buffalo to see her graduate. None of us ever made it past high school, so being on that stately campus impressed the hell out of all of us.

That evening we had dinner at a restaurant a couple of miles down the road from the school. My sister wasn't with us. She was hitting all of the graduation parties in her dorm. We wouldn't see her until the next morning. The restaurant was dark inside with wooden floors. It had wagon wheel lights overhead. The dining room was packed. We sat at a round table with heavy wooden chairs. We all ordered something different. I had a pork chop dinner with mashed potatoes and corn and my wife had a ham steak with the same. My Dad had meatloaf and his wife had fried chicken that looked pretty damn good. My brother had a steak and his mousy girlfriend had battered-fried fish. She picked the golden batter away from the fish and moved it to my brother's plate. He scarfed it down in big bites.

"That's the best part," he said, noisily smacking his greasy lips.

The old man was pounding red wine and his wife was throwing back scotch and sodas. Her face was melting and her eyes were glassy. The more my old man drank, the louder he got. My old man was a big man with a square face and thick hands. A few people at other tables glanced uneasily in our direction.

We got to talking about traveling and places we'd like to visit. My wife mentioned France.

"Paris is filthy," my old man said. "They let dogs shit inside the cafes. I wouldn't go back there for any-thing. The women stink too. They don't bathe as far as I can tell and their armpits are full of hair."

"I don't think all of Paris is that bad," I said.

"It's a shit hole," he said. "If you were ever there, you'd know."

"Jesus, Dan," his wife said, "Keep your voice down. You're too loud."

"Hey, I'm just saying, Paris is a shit hole. If you want to go somewhere good, then go to Ireland. The pubs there are great."

"Well for Christ sakes we're in a restaurant," she said.

My brother got rid of the grease shining brightly on his lips by wiping his sleeve across his mouth.

"The food in Ireland sucks," he said.

"What the hell do you know about the food in Ireland?" the old man said. "Ireland happens to be known for their salmon and hearty stews. It's better than that buttery French shit, turned my stomach when I was there. I had to shit for a week."

"The beer's good in Ireland," I said. "Guinness is good stuff, especially over there. It doesn't travel well, so by the time we get it here it tastes different."

"That, I agree with," my old man said. "The black pint is the best beer in the world and they have good goddamn whisky too. The Paddy and the Jameson, that's the good stuff. You can't drink the Bushmills though, that's Protestant shit. The Catholics won't touch it."

Once we were all finished with dinner, the waitress returned, cleared our plates and recited the dessert list. When she said the restaurant was serving cream puffs, my old man said he'd like to give her a cream puff of his own.

"For God's sake!" his wife said.

The old man thought he was pretty funny and let out a hearty laugh. My wife shot him a disgusted look and we all ordered a few desserts to pass around. We ordered a marble cheese cake, a piece of apple pie and one of those cream puffs with chocolate sauce. My old man insisted.

"What the hell are you looking at?" he asked my wife.

"Leave it go, Dan," his wife said. "You're too loud and rude."

"Why would you say something as crude as that?" my wife asked.

"Fuck it. Lighten up," he said.

The desserts came and we dug in and passed them around. In a moment they were gone and my old man ordered another bottle of wine. He ordered a scotch and soda for his wife.

"Just give me a scotch on the rocks," she said, her face melting. "The soda makes me belch."

My old man looked at his wife. "You're getting drunk again. Every fuckin' time," he said.

"Shove it," she said. "You don't tell me what to do. I'm certainly not drunk. Not as drunk as you're getting, anyway."

I was hoping the old man wouldn't do anything stupid tonight. It was going to be a big day for my sister and I was hoping he could keep it together, but I saw he was getting agitated by the narrowness of his eyes and the fact that he was tightening and puckering his lips.

My brother brought the conversation around to his girlfriend telling us she was going to open a flower shop.

"There's and empty store for rent on Hertel Avenue right next to that Greek restaurant and across from the row of antique shops. There's a bunch of other shops there too and between the foot traffic and the stuff she can sell on the computer, she should do okay."

"You can't make any money selling flowers," my old man said. "By the time you pay your overhead, there won't be any profit left. If you want to make money selling stuff, work at one of those pharmaceutical companies and sell drugs. With what they charge us for fucking medicine nowadays, you'll make a fortune."

"I can get a pretty good deal buying flowers wholesale," the Mouse said.

"You can't make shit," my old man insisted. "Are you going to deliver?"

"I don't know," the Mouse said. "I hadn't thought of that."

"Some plan," my old man said.

"For God's sake," my old man's wife said. "Let her do what she wants. Maybe she likes flowers."

"I do like flowers," the Mouse said.

The waitress returned to our table and asked if there was anything else she could get for us. She stood opposite from my old man. She was young and pretty and wore a stained apron over her uniform. She nervously clutched the check inside of a leather cover in her hand.

"No, you can't give me what I want so you better give the bill to me," my old man said. "We can drink the rest of this wine at the bar."

The old man paid the bill and I snuck another twenty into the leather book for her troubles.

A few heads from other tables turned in our direction. Their eyes followed my old man as he stumbled a little clumsily toward the bar with his glass in one hand and a bottle of red wine in the other. A few seats opened at the bar and we gave them to the ladies. A couple argued in loud whispers a few seats over and the woman had tears running down her cheeks.

"I wonder what's going on with them," my old man said, loudly looking in their direction.

"It's not our business, Dad," I said.

"I didn't say it's our damn business, but I'd sure like to know what they're yappin' about," he said.

An hour later we were the only ones at the bar. A few tables lingered in the dining room over dessert and coffee and the couple that was arguing had left. My old man ordered another bottle of wine and his wife was on another scotch. The rest of us were drinking Budweiser out of the bottle. The bartender wiped the bar clean. He laid some pretzels out in bowls before us. My wife was getting loud. She was hell-bent on fucking with my old man.

"All he wanted was to spend a little time with you and you left him in the hotel room and went out drinking with Jack," she said.

My brother Jack looked at me and shrugged.

"Fuck him," my old man said.

"Fuck your son? How nice," my wife said. "You know you can be a real piece of shit!"

"Relax," I said to my wife.

"You relax! He stiffed you and you tell me to re-lax?" she said.

"It doesn't matter," I said.

"Fuck him," my old man said, looking at me with those cold eyes and tight lips.

"Don't you ever say that to him again," my wife said.

"Fuck him!" my old man repeated.

My wife lunged at the old man and he raised his hand high following through with an open-palm smacking it hard against her face.

"Jesus Christ!" his wife screamed. "You're wrong, Dan! You're goddamned wrong!"

"Shut up, Eleanor!" my old man said.

My brother grabbed the Mouse and said, "I'm outta here!"

I grabbed my wife and pulled her out of the bar. "Let's get the hell out of here, too," I said.

The old man's hand print burned crimson red on her cheek. I suddenly felt sober and a little shaky. We got in the car and silently drove back to the hotel. I had nothing to say to my wife and she had nothing to say to me. She lit a cigarette and rolled down the window letting in cold, wet wind and I wanted to throw her out of the car. I could see the old man's headlights behind me and I could tell by how close he was riding my ass that he was madder than hell. We all pulled into the parking lot of the hotel at about the same time and I parked the car and went inside without looking back.

My brother and the Mouse were inside the lobby and the old man's wife came in a moment later.

"You're father's wrong," she said, in a syrupy slur. "He's goddamned wrong."

I could see my wife letting the old man have it out in the parking lot. I could see her through the glass doors of the lobby. Her face pressing close to his, and I knew the old man going to snap at any moment.

"This is bullshit," I said, and headed toward the glass doors to drag my wife out from the parking lot and up to our room.

The old man's wife slid in front of me and put her arm out to hold me back saying, "Let 'em be for God's sake, they've got to figure it out."

I pushed past her and my brother followed me telling the old man, "Jesus, he almost knocked Eleanor down trying to get at you, Dad."

The old man turned at me with cold eyes and clenched fists.

"You little fuck," he said. "You touch my wife and I'll kill you!"

"Christ, I didn't touch her," I said.

My old man moved toward me. I backed up and

found myself pinned against a car in the parking lot. I could hear his wife slurring, "Dan, for God's sake stop it, you're wrong!"

My old man grabbed my neck with his left hand and threw a couple of sloppy right hooks onto the side of my face. He had me close against the car and leaned into me spewing something about if I ever touch his wife he'd kill me. His eyes were narrow and his breath stunk like wine and cigarettes and I could smell that shitty cologne he douses himself with. Spit flew from his mouth and I realized at that moment how weak the old man was. He kept his hand on my neck and made a couple of feeble attempts to knee me in the balls and I realized that this guy, who I had always feared as being one tough son-of-a-bitch, was a weak pitiful man who could not hurt me no matter how hard he tried. It was a realization that made me a bit sad. The old man swore up and down and finished his tirade by spitting in my face. I pushed him off of me, wiped the slime from my face, grabbed my wife, and dragged her through the lobby and toward the elevator. In the distance I could hear my brother talking to the pimply-faced kid at the front desk saying something like, "You don't have to worry about getting the cops here; we'll go to our rooms and quiet down. You won't hear no more from us."

*****

The next morning, I woke with a painful cloudy head and a swollen throat. My wife sat at the foot of the bed smoking a joint and brushing shiny red polish onto her toes. The clock-radio on the side of the bed blared Aerosmith's *Love in an Elevator*. She had made a cup of weak coffee in the little coffee pot on the table next to the television.

"Drink that," she said, pointing to the cup of watered down crap. "You need to put on that shirt and tie and we need to get going. The graduation starts in a half hour."

We arrived at the Escoffier dining room. Big round tables with white table cloths were packed tightly next to one another, and a huge chandelier hung in the center of the impressive room. My wife and I were the first to arrive. She wore a short white dress with red high-heeled shoes. As the room filled, my brother and the Mouse arrived, followed by my old man and his wife. Finally, my sister met us at the table wearing a flower patterned dress and a wide smile.

"Isn't this great?" she said, her eyes bright. "I can't believe I'm actually graduating. It's so cool. We were all out late last night going from one room to another and having an awesome party. I only slept for about an hour, but I'm not even tired."

My old man wouldn't look in my direction. His wife focused on me and mustered a weak good morning. Her eyes were two slits. She sipped her coffee with shaky hands. My old man looked great. None of those hard nights ever took a toll on him. He snapped back the next morning without any problems. He was loud and commented on what a *fancy-assed* place this was and that he hadn't had a neck tie on since Uncle Jack, *that piece of shit*, died and we had to go to his *fuckin' funeral*. My brother and the Mouse were in fine spirits, too. My brother sat down and started gorging on a plate of sweet-rolls placed in the center of the table.

"Save some of those for the rest of us," my old man grumbled.

After breakfast we took some pictures with the seven of us standing in a semi-circle around the table. A black man in a brown shark-skinned suit sitting at the next table took some shots from each of our cameras. The old man and I were at opposite ends of the table with my sister, dead center, beaming into the camera. Once that was done, we headed to the graduation ceremony.

The graduation hall was ornate with white scrolled walls and stained glass windows. We found seats in separate sections of the room. After a short wait, the graduates strolled in wearing wide smiles, and uniformed in black pants, crisp-white chef coats and tall toque chef hats. A gold medal with yellow ribbon hung proudly from their necks.

A slender man, in full chef's regalia, who served as the head chef at the White House for something like twenty years, spoke to the graduates telling them they were going to make a big difference in the world if they worked hard and stayed focused. He told them they needed to accept challenges, and there were many challenges in this business. He said he was born in Switzerland and spoke in a soft voice with a thick accent. Another chef in a stiff white chef's coat and toque moved to the podium, congratulated the new graduates, and announced the prestigious Culinary Institute Graduate Awards. My sister grabbed two of the three. I clapped very hard when they called her name and I felt my throat tightening as she got up from her seat and took those awards. I thought, "She's going to make it out of the shit back in Buffalo. She can go anywhere in the world she wants."

*****

After the ceremony, my wife and I drove from Hyde Park along a curved road through dry, leafless woods. The day was gray with no sun. I didn't say much along the drive, but I knew I had to leave my wife. It wasn't going to work out. I wasn't sure how or when or even why, but I knew it needed to end. I knew she caused me too much trouble.

I remember the mostly long silence during the rest of that drive and thinking about the absurdity of my old man's behavior and how that once strong man had regressed into pathetic weakness. Maybe I found strength in that. It really was a funny thought.

ANTONIO GIANNI
DI MARCO

I t was seven o'clock in the morning and Antonio Gianni Di Marco woke abruptly from a dream that left him hollow and yearning for days long gone. He lay in bed in the heavy stillness of his dark room straining to piece together the details of the dream, something about his wife stopping by the train station in Buffalo on her way to Los Angeles and begging him to come with her. It was a strange dream because neither Antonio nor his wife had ever been to Los Angeles. In the dream she was very young, about the same age as when they were married. Her face was smooth as porcelain and dark chestnut eyes welled with tears. She tried to persuade him to go to Los Angeles telling him it is always sunny in California, never dark and cloudy like it is in Buffalo.

"That was probably fifty years ago," he thought. It was all very strange and real. "How long had she been dead?" He tried to remember. "Six years? Seven?" He had to think for a moment, had to shake off the sleepiness, the loneliness, the dream. "Of course," he remembered –

Angelina had been gone ten years.

The dream followed him, holding on cloudy and uneasy in his head.

At eighty-four, Antonio still had some definition in his biceps; his legs were firm, and he never developed a flabby, round stomach like just about everyone else he knew. He had a good head of thick grey hair, still streaked with threads of black that he combed back from his forehead. His legs and shoulders were stiff in the morning which prompted his ritual of rising slowly from his bed and stretching until his muscles loosened and he could move more easily. He was proud of his body, but his face was lined and furrowed, dried and spotted like a brittle autumn leaf. He shuffled into the bathroom looking into the mirror thinking, "Who is that man?"

The dream refused to leave him, gripping deeply into the abyss of his soul. Antonio stirred about the soundless rooms, his heart fluttering rapidly, a pervasive uneasiness enveloping him.

After brushing his teeth and shaving, Antonio moved into the living room, pushed aside the curtain, and watched from his window the busy street below. He lived above a Puerto Rican grocery store on Niagara Street in a red-brick building he owned and raised his family in. His children were grown. Anna moved to San

Francisco with her girlfriend and worked at some big time marketing agency. Tony sold real-estate and lived in a gigantic house with his wife in North Buffalo. They both left the neighborhood many years earlier. Left it to the Puerto Ricans who took over the Lower West Side sending the Italians fleeing to North Buffalo and eventually the suburbs, left them sharing it now with Africans, Muslims, West Indian's, and colorful transplants from Burma.

The dream lingered ominously throughout the morning. It triggered nostalgia for the past forcing upon him a heavy desire to erase the guilt-ridden thoughts that contaminated his mind. These thoughts generated shame and uneasiness that he carried with him year after year.

Looking from his window at Niagara Street below, Antonio remembered the early years, the sweet smell of bread baking in backyards from coal-fired brick ovens. He remembered, as a boy, lugging wooden crates of dark-purple-skinned grapes into his parent's cellar and using crude presses to crush the grapes and make the deep ruby-purple wine. Just about every family in the neighborhood made this dark, dry wine and drank it with their nightly macaroni and sauce. Throughout many homes on the West Side, cured hams and homemade pork sausages seasoned with parsley, oregano, and salty parmesan hung in dry attics.

He remembered the wooden and brick homes on the west side of Niagara Street that had been wiped away, bulldozed over, one dwelling at a time, in the name of *urban renewal*. That's what Mayor Sedita called it in nineteen fifty-eight when he gave the go ahead to demolish the neighborhood that ran between City Hall and Columbus Hospital. It was the beginning of the end. The only place spared was the church of St. Anthony of Padua, its red-brick steeple rising into the sky helplessly watching the carnage. That was the time when most of the Italians were swindled into taking meager compensations for their homes, moving from the comfort of their celebrated culture and identity to unfamiliar areas beyond. They moved into neighborhoods founded by the Irish, Polish, Germans, and the Jews.

Possibly, if Antonio's home and paint store had been on the west side of Niagara Street, he too would have left. But, his place was on the east side of the street and he was spared the wrath of angry bulldozers knocking his neighborhood into a new, alien, and foreign land. As the years pressed forward Antonio learned to live on a street now plagued with shootings, robberies, and drug dealings.

In a neighborhood where once the long, lyrical

vowels of Italian drifted from neighbor to neighbor on the crowded streets, Antonio succumbed to the new sounds of rapid-fire Spanish and now the strange guttural sounds of Arabic and other languages he could not identify. Yet, he never left. He continued living in this strange land as a ghost, a relic of days gone by.

*****

For many years the grocery was Antonio's paint store. He opened it in nineteen fifty-five and kept it running until nineteen ninety-five when he rented it out to Angel Ortiz, a hard-working second generation Puerto Rican, who had tough luck doing business. By then the neighborhood had become unrecognizable. Nobody was buying anything from the small shops on Niagara Street anymore. Butcher shops, bakeries, seafood shops, delicatessens, all caved into the mega stores opening away from the neighborhood. Niagara Street was nothing more than a dilapidated, shattered, lonely dream.

Antonio paid cash for the paint store in nineteen fifty-five, a perk for being connected to the Marinelli family. He never intended to work for Stefano Marinelli, it just, like all other things, happened.

Antonio sat in the quiet room looking at the street below and thought, perhaps, if he had never had that first encounter with Stefano Marinelli, then maybe, he would not have carried this burden with him, this dark stain that clung so nightmarishly onto his soul. The dream he carried with him on this morning reminded him of that.

*****

In nineteen fifty-two, Antonio and his brother Franco worked together as painters. It was arduous work and long hours produced a meager income. They worked for the Italians in the neighborhood and were known to do excellent work at a fair price. They always had enough work and got their jobs through word of mouth as was the way things were done on the West Side in those days. At the time, Antonio rented the paint shop from Silvio Grimaldi, a sharp businessman who owned many properties along Niagara Street. They owned a step van with *Di Marco Painting* stenciled in bold red on each side. It was in that van that they loaded their ladders, pails of paint, and brushes.

It happened that Marinelli needed someone to paint his kitchen in his home up in the Town of Lewiston, by the Lower Niagara River. Marinelli's cousin recommended Antonio, and he and Franco loaded the van and headed to do the job. When they arrived, Marinelli himself in a grey suit and black tie greeted them at the door. He looked out at the driveway and took special note of the van.

Antonio and Franco surveyed the kitchen and quoted a price of $25.00.

"It's a fair price," Marinelli said.

The two worked in their diligent manner and completed the job in a couple of hours.

"It's beautiful work," Marinelli said. "My cousin Antonella Barone, she lives on 7th Street in Buffalo, my cousin, she tells me Antonio and Franco Di Marco, they will do a good job for you."

"We know Antonella very well," Antonio said.

"She comes from Castellammare del Golfo like we do," Franco said.

"It's a small world," Stefano Marinelli said. "We are all from the same town. It was many years ago I left Castellammare del Golfo. It was in nineteen-nine. I was only a boy of eighteen."

"We were young too," Antonio said. "I was six and Franco was only four when we came over. I have never been back, but maybe someday I would like to see it, who knows."

"You have done a beautiful job on the kitchen. I am hoping I can convince you to paint my living room and dining room. I would appreciate that greatly," Marinelli said.

"It's no problem Signor Marinelli," Antonio said. "We can come back in the morning, tomorrow. We have a job we have to do this afternoon and then we can be here tomorrow."

"Bene," Marinelli said. "Keep your appointment for today. I will look for you in the morning."

*****

The following morning Antonio and Franco pulled their van into the driveway of Stefano Marinelli's home. Marinelli greeted them at the door wearing a black suit with an open-collared white shirt. The walls in the living room and dining room where bare and the furniture was pushed to the middle of the rooms and covered with large sheets of canvas.

"You have done half the work for us, Signor Marinelli," Antonio said.

"I hired you to paint, not move furniture," Marinelli said. "I have others to move furniture. You do not need to be bothered with that."

"Grazie, Signore Marinelli," Franco said. "You make our job easy."

"Prego," Marinelli said, with a wave of his hand. "Everybody has a job, a place. When everyone works together we get things done…the right way."

"I understand," Franco said.

Again, Antonio and Franco painted the rooms with quickness and precision. They loaded their supplies back into the van and met with Stephano Marinelli for payment. Marinelli gave them two crisp one hundred dollar bills.

"Signor Marinelli," Antonio said, "we agreed on one hundred dollars as a total, not one for each of us."

"I understand," Marinelli said, "but the work you do is better than any of the men who have done jobs for me. You are fair and efficient and your work is thorough and very well done. It is a testament to who you are."

"Grazie, Signor Marinelli," Antonio and Franco replied.

"Prego," Marinelli said, and studied the men before him. "I could use two men like you to help me with a service. It requires the use of your step van to make deliveries when needed. I need friends who can pay attention to details and are efficient like you two have demonstrated. I will pay very well for your services and word of your confidentiality."

"What kind of work do you have in mind, Signor Marinelli?" Antonio asked.

"It's a simple job of receiving and delivering," Marinelli said. "I will have one of my associates let you know where to pick up a delivery to take to your paint store where you will prepare it for delivery at another place. My associate's name is Nicolo Leone. He will give you all of the directions you need if you choose to work for me. You will be paid well for your services."

Antonio looked for a sign of benevolence in Marinelli's eyes and found none. Those dark eyes held onto Antonio with complacent firmness as he awaited an answer. Antonio knew a decision needed to be made quickly, that much money could be made, but at a great risk.

"If you beg my pardon, Signor Marinelli," Antonio continued. "My brother and me, we have lived a simple way by painting the houses of people we know, by building our business a little bigger each year. We don't want to lose what we started. I am recently married and want to start a family with my wife, Angelina. How great are the risks, Signor Marinelli?"

"There are always risks in business, Antonio," Marinelli said. "You know this as well as me, but men with your skills can be very helpful, and can make very good money if they do it right. You and your wife, Angelina will have the money to make a very comfortable living."

Marinelli excused himself for a moment and came back with ten crisp one hundred dollar bills.

"You take this and think about our arrangement," Marinelli said. "If you chose not to, then you keep this as a tip for your fine work. I will understand. I will send Nicolo to visit you tomorrow for and answer.

*****

The next day Nicolo Leone arrived at the paint store. Nicolo was a large man with a wide head and bushy eyebrows. He did not appear to Antonio like a man of patience or one that took pleasure in negotiating.

"Well, what will it be?" Nicolo asked. "Mr. Marinelli is waiting for your answer."

Antonio looked at Franco and then into the vacant eyes of Nicolo Leone, "Tell Signor Marinelli it will be a privilege to work for him."

"Bene," Nicolo said. "There is a shoe repair shop at 1226 Niagara Street. Be there at eleven o'clock tonight, park on the side of the building, and when you see a light flick on and off once, come quietly into the door on the side.

"Bene," Antonio said.
"Bene," Franco said.

*****

Antonio and Franco were punctual. Men of their word. They pulled the van to the side of the building, turned off the headlights, and waited for a signal. The light flicked once as planned and Antonio and Franco slid into the building through the side door. Nicolo Leone and another man with sinister eyes and bloody hands motioned for them to follow through a dim hallway and into the main room of the shoe repair shop. The smell of shoe wax and leather hung in the air. In the center of the room covered under a dark wool blanket lay the figure of a body. The head was wrapped with a blanket and a wet stain widened in a dark purple before them. At the other end of the body, a shiny pair of patent-leather shoes gleamed in the shadowy room.

"I have written down your instructions on how and where to deliver the body," Nicolo Leone said, handing Antonio a folded sheet of paper. "It will be the same every time. It is done under the careful direction of Mr. Marinelli. You might say it is his personal calling card."

Antonio and Franco carried the body through the dark hallway and in through the back door of the step van. Beads of perspiration hung on Antonio's lip as he struggled with the awkward heaviness of the dead man. Nicolo Leone put a five-gallon pail with a bag of powdered concrete into the van with the body.

"The directions are clear," he said. "Follow them precisely as they are written."

"Bene," Antonio said with difficulty.

"Bene," Franco said, and drove from the shoe repair shop to their paint store.

When Antonio and Franco reached the paint store, they lugged the body through the side door and into the back storage room where they stored cans of paint on shelves. There were no windows in the storage room so turning on the light would not cause any suspicion. Antonio read the directions as Franco unwrapped the blanket from the dead man. His face bloody and mashed, like raw hamburger, with broken crooked teeth and lifeless bulbous eyes protruding from an agonizing snarl.

"Holy Jesus," Antonio gasped, when he saw the mangled face before him. Antonio and Franco knew immediately they had made a horrible decision, knew immediately the power and wrath of Stephano Marinelli, and knew immediately there was no way out from what they had agreed to.

Antonio and Franco worked methodically, diligently. Antonio prayed silently to himself as he mixed the concrete into the pail, added water to get the consistency to a malleable paste so he and Franco could apply it onto the dead man's shiny shoes, and up to his knees. While they waited for the concrete to harden, Antonio thought of Angelina upstairs sleeping soundly, unaware of the horror below. He had told her his first lie that night, told her that he and Franco met a man from Castella-mmare del Golfo, a good man, who was a manager in a warehouse that made paint. Antonio told Angelina if he worked sometimes in the evenings he would be paid by getting his paint for free. It would cut costs greatly and they would make more money; they could purchase the store from Silvio Grimaldi, he told her. Antonio told An-gelina many lies after that. Many lies to keep her safe.

When the concrete was dry enough, Antonio and Franco lugged the body back into the step van. They drove without speaking through the hushed city streets to the foot of Ferry Street, past the black-steel draw bridge, and under a cluster of elm trees where they entered the body into the Niagara River. They did this as often as Stephano Marinelli requested; there were no other choices but to fulfill his wishes.

Under a starless purple-black sky, before the body was let into the cold tumultuous current of the Niagara River, Antonio constructed a tiny cross made from two sticks and some string he had in his van. He whispered The Lord's Prayer and placed the cross securely into the hand of the dead man, something he would do for the rest of the years and the rest of the dead men.

*****

The dream reminded Antonio that all things pass.

Angelina, Franco, Marinelli, Nicolo Leone were long dead, reduced to fine dust and bones, their bodies a material now indescribable. All of them buried with oppressive secrets that haunted them when they walked this earth looking for some impression of purpose.

Angelina knew all along, Antonio thought. How could she not? All of those late nights secretly sliding in and out of the paint shop doors with Franco. Antonio recalled those surreptitious nights, he and Franco never speaking to one another, just carrying out the specific written instructions that Marinelli handed to Nicolo Leone, who handed them to Antonio and Franco with a watchful nod and dark warning eyes. The instructions were to be burned after each job. Everything was better left unsaid.

In the dream Angelina pleaded for Antonio to come with her, to come to her stripped clean of the furtive dark-ness that clung to his soul. Antonio realized there was only one way out.

Antonio walked steadily down the back stairs

from his flat, through the back stock room, and into the grocery where Angel Ortiz was stocking canned goods onto shelves.

"You have a fine store, Angel," Antonio said. "You keep working hard and this business will grow."

"Thank you, Mr. Antonio," Angel replied. "I can only hope it will be as good as yours once was."

"Angel, I hope you can believe me when I tell you, your store is much better. It is an honest business and you are an honest man."

"Gracias, Mr. Antonio," Angel said.

Antonio walked out from the grocery and headed down Niagara Street to St. Anthony of Padua Church. Along the way he noticed some of the abandoned store fronts had been swept out, their windows cleaned, signs of rebirth.

He reached the church and entered through the big wooden doors adorned with black iron handles. He noticed a sign on the vestibule that read *Pastor Fred Davies*.

"He's not even Italian," Antonio thought. "Maybe it's a good thing."

Inside the church a few people knelt in prayer in scattered pews waiting their turn in the confessional. The church was silent and when a woman coughed it echoed dryly throughout the cavernous room. Antonio sat in a pew and waited. He felt Angelina's presence and it gave him comfort. When it was his turn, Antonio entered the confessional and sat on a wooden chair. He waited until Father pushed aside a screen revealing a shadowy silhouette.

"In the name of the Father, the Son and the Holy Spirit. Amen."

Antonio followed Father's words with the sign of the cross, leaned forward and began, "Bless me Father for I have sinned…"

A Brief
Encounter

He imagined the slim good-looking ones who wore tight, white pants and white t-shirts with slicked black hair and shiny black shoes. He imagined the single men or the bolder pairs who walked the ashen, brick streets in the warm evenings searching for *las turistas*. He thought of the bull-fighters or anyone who worked in the ring from the *picadors* to the *banderilleros* to the *matadors,* and wondered who she had the encounter with.

Thomas was vacationing with his girlfriend, Nancy. They were doing their best to ignite a dismal, hopeless relationship. Nancy desired a lot. She had insatiable sexual cravings. It took more than he had to satisfy her and she was rarely content. He lit a cigarette, feeling worthless.

They stood on the sidewalk looking through the big window of a busy tapas bar and decided it was too packed to go inside. It was nine o'clock and the cafes and restaurants were filled. Madrid was alive on this gentle summer night. They strolled down the crowded, narrow street. Tom walked close to Nancy, her arm tucked under his. There were many signs and lights on the cafes and shops. Under a low-hanging, resplendent, bone-colored moon, a mild breeze pushed scents of food and *cerveza* through the ancient streets.

"I remember earlier walking by a small café around the corner," Nancy said. "We can have a coffee and maybe it won't be very crowded."

They walked past a butcher shop that was just closing, and a *pension* with massive dark green shutters called *Hostel El Pilar.* Finally, they reached the café. They walked in and it was not crowded. A large woman with a perspiring forehead stood wearily behind the counter. She had doughy arms and tiny black eyes. On the other side of the counter sat a very old and very slim man in a worn grey suit with black, scuffed, lace-up shoes. His legs were long and crossed over one another. His shoulders were bony and slouched, supporting a long neck and pointed face.

"*Dos café con leche, por favor,*" Thomas said, reaching into his pocket for a 5 *Euro* note. The woman took his money, made the coffees quickly, and set them on the counter.

"*Gracias,*" Thomas said.

"*De nada,*" replied the woman.

"I'm sorry, Tom," Nancy said.

"I don't want to talk about it," Thomas said.

The woman behind the counter slid her flabby arm across her forehead, wiping away tiny beads of perspiration. The slim man looked up toward Thomas, then quickly lowered his head and muttered into his coffee cup.

"Let's go back to our room, Nancy," Thomas said.

As they walked slowly down the street and through the *Puerta del Sol,* past the lights and cafes, Thomas imagined all types of Spanish men. He knew she could not be trusted. He had hoped a trip would work; a trip to Spain, an exotic place, somewhere different than where they had come from. A place where, perhaps, she would think only of him.

They reached their pension and climbed the three floors of worn, wooden steps to their door at the end of the hall. Once inside, Nancy sat on a wooden-spindled chair in front of a large mirror and combed her hair in long delicate sweeps. Tears flowed in tiny rivulets over her cheeks. Thomas stood behind her and placed his hands lightly on her shoulders. He looked at their reflection in the mirror.

This would not work. Nothing would ever work. Not now, not later.

Later in the evening Thomas woke from an uneasy sleep. Outside the breeze swirled slightly cooler through the sleepy city. Thomas lit a cigarette and roamed the now silent and narrow streets. On the *Puerta del Sol* two men swept the giant square with big push-brooms, and then hosed it down for the following day.

In the small café the perspiring woman wiped the counter and switched off the lights. The slim man was sleeping deeply and snoring lightly, alone in his small room. Nancy lay in the moonlit room sleeping peacefully with her mouth slightly open and her eyes dry.

The Diner

W e had good luck catching rides out of Tampa and up Interstate 75. After a couple of hours we made it to Interstate 10, just outside of Live Oaks, Florida and headed west. It was cloudy and humid. Thick air hung low to the ground. Traffic was sparse. I leaned against the guardrail and read Hemingway's *Indian Camp*, a beautiful and sad story about growing up. Michael stood nearby silently juggling rocks and throwing his thumb out when a possible ride approached. We didn't talk very much.

Our first lift came from a young black dude who took us across Interstate 10 to Oakdale, a city west of Tallahassee. The ride was long and dull. Interstate 10 through northwest Florida between Tallahassee and Pensacola is an endless monotony of four straight lanes cutting through rows and rows of endless pines, mile after mile. Long stretches without exits are common and only a sluggish ripple of hills break up the dullness a bit. The road is sparsely populated. The towns in between are small and few.

The black dude dropped us off at a tiny Hopperesque diner with a tattered sign hanging over the front door that read, *Home of the World's Best Fried Chicken.* A bell was attached to the door. It jingled as we entered. It was quiet inside. Two ceiling fans stirred the hot, dead air. A horsefly buzzed angrily throughout the room. An old black man sat alone at the counter spooning sugar into a tall mug of coffee. He sat bent over a huge piece of apple pie; a bunch of napkins lay scattered in front of him. He looked in our direction, nodded, and went back to spooning the sugar steadily into his coffee. I could smell grease from the fryer. At a booth sat two teenage girls wearing skimpy shorts and halter-tops. They were drinking Cokes and sharing a basket of fries. Behind the counter, next to the register, a tired woman in a white waitress uniform filled the salt and pepper shakers that lined the counter with the tops off. She used a paper funnel to fill each one. Behind the counter and in the kitchen, an old wire-thin black man, with gray kinky hair, prepped his workstation by chopping potatoes and throwing them in a big oiled skillet with onions. The pan sizzled when the potatoes hit the skillet. He wore a Miami Dolphins cap and looked down at his work. This was the quiet time between lunch and dinner. We grabbed a booth in the front of the restaurant that looked out over the gravel parking lot. Our packs rested against the seat and under the table. The interstate stretched long and lonely in the distance. The big horsefly landed on our table roving aimlessly over the yellowed linoleum.

The waitress wiped her brow with the back of her hand, put the shakers aside, and walked towards our booth. She carried a pungent, stale scent of cigarette tobacco with her. The two girls looked up from their Cokes and watched her approach us. Michael caught the eye of the pretty little one in the yellow halter, and winked at her. They smiled bashfully, lowered their heads, and concentrated on the basket of fries before them.

There were no menus. Over the counter, on a big sign, was a list of items: Fried Chicken in a Basket $2.99. Hamburger $1.49, Cheeseburger $1.59, Fries .79, Coffee, Coke…the usual stuff.

"What can I get for ya'all?"

Michael looked towards the sign. "How's that chicken in the basket?"

"Best around, but it ain't gonna be ready for 'bout half hour. We cook it fresh."

"Sure. That's okay." He looked at me. "You care?"

"No. I'm good." I ordered the same along with an iced Coke.

The waitress looked at our packs. "Where you boys headin'?"

"We started off in Buffalo and are hoping to get into New Orleans in the next day or so," Michael responded.

"Good times over there," she reflected, walking back to the counter. "Two in the basket, Jess." She poured coffee for the old timer working through the pie, then pulled out a long slender cigarette from her apron, lit it, and returned to the salt and pepper shakers.

Michael grabbed a Marlboro from a side pocket in his back pack and lit it.

"Doesn't look like much goes on around here," he said.

"Not much," I agreed, taking the Rand McNally from my pack and spreading it before us. "We still have a way to go before we get to New Orleans. It looks like we'll be sleeping in a field around here unless we get a night ride out."

"We need to find a truck stop and get a ride. I don't want to sleep in some field," Michael said.

The waitress returned with two iced Cokes in tall sweaty glasses that said Coca-Cola on the sides. She set them before us and laid our silverware down. The fan whirred; the air was thick and heavy. A white Chevy

Nova with a black top pulled into the parking lot. It could be a ride out of here, I thought. Two men got out of the car and headed towards the door. The bell jingled when the two men entered. The one carefully closed the door. It appeared the jingle annoyed him.

The first man was short with bowed legs, and a thick head of wavy hair. His eyes were mismatched. His left eye almost permanently shut. He wore about a week's worth of stubble on his face. The second was tall and stupid looking with a large wide forehead and deep almond brown eyes. They wore blue jeans and western shirts. The tall one kept his unbuttoned. The stupid looking man glanced pensively at us, then at the waitress, and then at the two girls who had lost their smiles and fidgeted with the straws in their Cokes. The short one asked the waitress how far town was from here.

"'bout two miles up the road," she answered.

"That's good," the man said. He looked at the stupid one fixated on the two girls. "Hey, ain't that good?"

"Yeah, boy," the tall one said.

The short man pointed to the kitchen. "Who's the fella with the Dolphin's cap?"

"That's Jess. He does the cookin'. Famous for makin' the best chicken anywhere around."

"Is that right?"

The waitress could not look into the short man's eyes. She turned slightly away and asked if he and his friend would like to sit at the counter or would they prefer a booth.

The man at the counter with the pie coughed and rose from his seat. The short one took a step forward and leaned into him.

"You just sit back down there, old feller. You ain't goin nowhere right now."

"Hey, what's doin'?" the waitress asked.

"You just lean against that counter and tell that old Jess to get his ass out here pronto," the short one said.

Jess dragged a dead leg reluctantly from the back of the pick-up counter and showed himself. He stood before the two men scared and trying to look dignified. The stupid one sat in the booth next to the pretty girl in the yellow halter and leaned into her. He whispered into her ear. She trembled and peed right there in the booth. When the stupid one felt the warm liquid penetrating his pants he smiled and stood up. Then he looked at Michael and me.

The waitress spoke clearly. "Look, this here is a little place. We ain't got hardly nothing in the register. Take it and leave us be."

The short one with the eyes that could not look

straight grabbed her forcefully by the arm and dragged her to the counter.

"You shut your damn trap and sit right here." He looked towards Jess. "You too, boy, sit your ass down next to her."

The short one needed to think for a moment while the stupid one stood slack-jawed waiting for directions. The short one looked at us.

"You two dumb asses; git up here, now."

The stupid one ushered us to the counter. Through his open shirt, I noticed the chocolate brown handle of a pistol resting in his pants and on his hip. The two girls were moved to the counter. They moved carefully towards us, and the stupid one took the palm of his hand and rested it on the girl with the yellow halter's ass feeling the wetness from her shorts. He looked at his hand and caressed his palm with his fingers cupping his hand to his nose and taking in the scent.

So there we were all sitting in a row at the counter, all silent except for the faint whimpering of the two girls and that damn angry horsefly.

The short one got behind the counter and faced us while the stupid one lurched menacingly from behind. We were sandwiched. The short one pointed to the waitress.

"Move your ass over and open that thing."

She moved quickly to the register and punched a key. The drawer opened with a thud and the ring of a bell.

"Ain't but seventy-five dollars in here," she said.

She pulled the small wad out carefully and handed it to the short one. The stupid one hung behind eyeballing the girl in the yellow halter.

"That ain't shit," the short one said. "What kind of place is this that ain't got money in the register?"

"We don't get much business till dinner time," the waitress said. "I guess you're better off robbin' us after the dinner shift," she said.

"Shut your mouth!" the short one said.

The short one glanced at the stupid one. For a moment he stood thinking. The stupid one lumbered directly behind the frightened girl in the yellow halter. He rested his hands firmly on each of her shoulders, and leaned into her ear.

"Why don't you get up and show me what the back of that kitchen looks like," he whispered.

Michael nudged me with his leg and shot a glance downward. He was holding a small hatchet he had taken out of his pack before we were brought up to the counter. He shot his eyes toward the big stupid one and then his eyes directed me to take care of the short one with the screwed up eyes. The stupid one lifted the girl from the counter to her feet. She was trembling and could barely stand. She whimpered, "No…please."

"Come on, now," he said guiding her away from the counter and towards the back.

The short one with the mismatched eyes smiled and I could see that his teeth were black and brown with big spaces between them. I noticed, on the counter, a large glass cylinder filled with sugar and for a moment everything stood still. Silence. Then, in one great and powerful motion, Michael pulled the hatchet from under the counter, cocked his arm like a pitcher releasing a fast ball, and hurled the hatchet at the tall stupid one with the blade tearing at the muscle under his left shoulder. He turned and in an instant Michael lowered his head and rammed the stupid one into the ground removing his pistol from his waist and shoving it hard into his mouth. At that moment, I lunged over the counter, grabbed the sugar container and smashed it against the side of the short one's head. He dropped to the ground, and like an insane alley cat, the waitress pounced on the short one and slammed his head repeatedly onto the tile floor screaming "You bastard, you fucking bastard!" The two girls high-tailed out of the restaurant and for a moment everything remained silent.

Michael cocked the hammer on the pistol and forced it further into the stupid one's mouth. Blood flowed down his chin and he choked on broken teeth.

Old Jess' hands shook and he pulled a set of keys from his pocket. "Put them in the walk-in cooler," he said. "It's got a lock on it."

The short one was out cold. The waitress dragged him by his feet into the walk-in cooler. Michael told the stupid one to get up. The stupid one told Michael to fuck-off and said he wasn't "gettin' in any cooler." Michael shot him in the foot and kicked him inside. Old Jess slammed the door shut and nervously locked the outside with a Master lock.

"Jesus Christ," Michael said. "That was fucking wild. Who are those guys?"

The waitress hurried toward the phone and frantically dialed a number.

"Get down to the diner pronto, Sheriff. Bring some boys with you because we got two crazy fuckers locked in the cooler and one's been shot in the foot!"

Sirens cut into the hot afternoon. The sheriff showed about fifteen minutes before the ambulance arrived. The ambulance had to come quite a distance from the hospital. The two girls came back once they figured it was safe and then, joined by the waitress, they told the sheriff the whole story.

The sheriff looked at Michael and me. He was a fat man with dark sunglasses and a big hat.

"Well, goddamn. I do believe we got us a couple of super-heroes."

And that's how we were treated…like a couple of super-heroes. And for the next five days we held up right there in Oakdale so the sheriff and the district attorney and guys from the FBI and all the curious town folks could get the facts straight and figure out what needed to be done with the legal system and all. The sheriff put us up in a creaky old hotel room right in the middle of town and the owner of the diner who was home napping when it all went down told us to "Order up boys any time, cause it's all on the house," and the two pretty girls came to our room with a bottle of sweet apple wine and we sat on the worn floor of this old beat up room, with the rays of the sun slanting in from an open window, cross-legged and playing poker and rummy and Michael showed them card tricks, and the pretty one who wore the yellow halter that day sat close to Michael so their shoulders touched and he held her hand gently and made her laugh often. Both girls smiled and smelled like fresh cut wheat.

The FBI let us know that these two were a traveling

pair of serial killers. The short one with the half closed eye was admitting to killing hundreds throughout the South. Said he had bodies buried everywhere. Said he'd been traveling with the stupid one for quite sometime now and they'd done a whole bunch of killin'. Newspaper reporters from all over the country came too. They took pictures of the diner. They took a picture with Old Jess and the waitress standing in front of the walk-in cooler. Old Jess holding up the padlock like you would hold up a big fat prize catfish. They even tried to interview the old man who muttered into his coffee cup. There wasn't much luck in that.

CHANGE iS
Good

I sat on a wooden chair in the school's office waiting for my daughter. I thought back to a day in nineteen seventy-five, walking home from St. Rose of Lima School for lunch. It was one of those odd early spring days. A blanket of snow covered the ground, but the temperature had strangely climbed above sixty degrees. I did everything I could to avoid getting my shoes wet, overstepping rivulets of water crisscrossing the sidewalk from the fast melting snow. I had on my green plaid jumper with the SRL insignia on it. I left my jacket at school and put on a navy blue sweater. That's all I needed. It was that nice outside. I walked home alone. The school let the eighth grade students out five minutes before the other grades.

"It's a privilege," our principal, Sister Jean told us.

I have five brothers. At the time, two were in high school and the other three went to St. Rose with me.

Somedays I waited for my brothers, but on that day I was very hungry and rushed to get home first and see what my mother was making for lunch. The back door was open and the screen wasn't locked. When I walked into the kitchen, she was using a spatula to flip pieces of Spam in the electric frying pan. On the counter were a head of iceberg lettuce and a loaf of Wonder Bread. A man with an enormous square head and bulging arm muscles stood behind her, with his hands cupping her breasts, nuzzling and kissing her neck. My mother wore a comfortable smile and leaned back into his chest. I startled them both when the screen door cracked behind me.

"Oh, good God!" my mother said, turning in my direction.

I watched the color drain from her face turning it dull as a winter's afternoon. The man grunted and turned his massive head in my direction.

"Bob, you'd better go now," my mother said.

"Hey," Bob said, sliding by me.

We eyed one another and Bob left. My mother stood looking at the Spam and the lettuce and bread, twisting the end of her hair with a forced smile.

"Grab some mayonnaise and mustard from the fridge, honey," she said. "We'll talk about this later."

*****

Later that evening I sat in the bathroom, on the lid of the toilet, watching my mother get ready to go out for the evening with my father. They were going to a house party down the street at the Sweeny's place. She stood before the mirror in her underwear and bra combing apricot-blonde hair with a cylinder brush. Her legs and arms were long and slender and she had a slight paunch sagging over the top of her underwear.

"I know we should talk about what you saw earlier today, but now is just not the right time," my mother said, carefully applying eyeliner. "Besides, these kinds of things can't be easily explained and you're awfully young to understand it all."

"I'm not that young," I said. "I think I understand it pretty well. You're having an affair with another man. Is he married?

"No, he's not married and I don't think we should be talking about this right now. I need to get ready. Do you understand me?"

"I suppose, but I don't like this," I said.

"Well, I don't like it either," she said. "Don't say anything to your father about this, okay?"

"I won't."

She pulled out a tube of glossy-red lipstick and applied it carefully to full, relaxed lips. Then, she pressed her lips on a folded piece of tissue to get rid of smudges tossing the tissue into the wastepaper basket; a wastebasket that was forever filled with my mother's lip prints.

"Well, that's a good thing or we'd all be in a lot of trouble the way he's been lately."

Later that night I woke up to my father and mother yelling and screaming at one another as they had done so many times.

"If you don't like it, why don't you just get the hell out of here?" I heard my father yell.

"*Me*? Why, *you're* nuts! Why should *I* get out?" My mother shouted.

My youngest brother, Davy, climbed into bed with me. He was only seven and got scared when they carried on like that. They both yelled and struggled and knocked things around until they had exhausted all of the problems and blames they could muster up toward each other for one night.

When I went into the kitchen the next morning, my mother had the electric frying pan out. She was mixing batter for pancakes.

"Your father went to the Knights," she said. "Get the syrup out of the fridge, would you honey?"

The Knights for my father meant the Knights of Columbus on Delaware Avenue. He went there on Saturday mornings to play handball, take a steam, and drink Genesee Cream Ales with his buddies. Pounders, they called them. I never got to go there because it's a men's club. My brothers would go down and play basketball and lift weights. They'd swim in the pool and sit in the steam room. My brothers would tell me the men swam naked in the pool. Big, fat hairy guys with little dicks, they'd say.

My father was a handsome man with a confident personality. People liked him. He was the general manager of a big department store at 998 Broadway Street called Sattler's. Sometimes my dad would take me to work with him and I did everything in my power to keep up with his frantic pace moving from one department to another. The women admired him and brightened up when he stopped to chat with them. They couldn't keep their eyes off of him. I noticed when he looked at some of them a particular way, they blushed or chewed nervously on their lips.

*****

A couple of months after I had seen my mother in the arms of that muscled stranger, I was sitting in English class getting publically berated by Sister Patricia about my lack of grammar skills. That old nun always did have it out for me and she'd let me have it whenever she could. Sister Jean entered the room and signaled for me to gath-

er my stuff and come with her. I left the room and tried
to keep up as she waddled ahead of me moving through
the halls in fervent determination. I followed her down
the dark hallway to the office and was surprised to see my
mother looking extraordinarily pretty and particularly
lonely sitting in the chair with her arms folded and her
knees and ankles pressed tightly together. She wore a
delicate yellow sun dress and white sandals. She looked
out of place. Sister Jean wasn't keen on having students
removed from school before dismissal, but my mother
assured her a personal matter took precedence and that I
would catch up on any missed work. Sister Jean frowned
and we were gone.

My mother drove a huge maroon four-door nine-
teen-seventy Pontiac Catalina that my grandfather gave
her. You'd think she'd get lost behind that giant steering
wheel, but she glided that car around the city effortlessly.

"I want to take you somewhere," she said.

We drove with the windows open down Hertel
Avenue past shops and restaurants and bars until we
reached the marina where the street ends at the Niagara
River. The day was warm and sunny and the river pushed
a slight chilly breeze in our direction. Rows of cabin
cruisers and open bow runabouts sat moored with thick
ropes to wooden docks, rocking in a perpetual motion.

The deep-green Niagara River surged frantically beyond a break wall.

"Why are we here?" I asked.

"Follow me," she said, walking toward a large cabin cruiser.

The cruiser was a thirty-two foot wooden Trojan. It had a bright white hull and a stained wooden deck with a shiny metal railing surrounding the perimeter of the boat. It appeared that no one was aboard.

"Come on," my mother said. "We can hop aboard."

"Whose boat is this?" I asked. "Why are we here?"

"You remember a few weeks back, when you came into the kitchen and I was with that man, Bob?"

"Yes," I said.

"Well, he lives here. This is his home for now, anyway."

"But, why are we here?" I asked.

"You're growing up and you're going to have to start understanding things. Things that might not be too pleasant, but they are real anyway."

We got on board and my mother opened a small door leading into a cramped dark room that smelled of cedar and pine. Everything was neat and compartmentalized. My mother flicked on a light and I noticed a sleeping area in the front of the boat with drawers lining the perimeter of the room. A toaster and a small Mr. Coffee machine sat on a foldable linoleum table with cushioned seating on each side. A clean ashtray and a full carton of Lark cigarettes were the only other things on the table.

"Bob was married, and recently went through a divorce. For the time being he's living on this boat," my mother said. "It's a beautiful boat, isn't it?"

"I guess so," I said.

"He's different than your father," my mother said, opening drawers and showing me neatly folded flannel shirts and faded blue jeans. "He's more of a laid-back man. Bob doesn't wear suits like your father; he wears more casual clothes."

I thought of my father's closet with color coded suits and sports jackets draped neatly within. The floor of my father's closet lined with shiny black and brown shoes. He was meticulous about the shine on his shoes and I often watched him take out his wooden shine box and apply thick black or brown polish and thoroughly buff his shoes with a brush until you could almost see your reflection.

"I learned this in the Army," he said. "If our boots weren't shined perfectly, that sergeant would make us run laps until we dropped."

Bob's shoes were stacked unevenly on a small shelf.

They were dull and smaller than my fathers.

My mother and I sat at the table, the boat rocking gently underneath us.

"Your father is going to move into his own place," my mother said. "It'll happen shortly; in a couple of weeks."

"Are you going to live on this boat with Bob?" I asked.

"Of course not," she said. "We're staying in our home."

"Is Bob moving in?"

"No, not now," she said, and began to cry. She cried deeply and politely and was embarrassed. "I don't know what is going to happen. It's all shit."

Growing up, I had seen my mother in the torrents of many emotions: happy and laughing, angry and nervous, bored and embarrassed. I had seen her eager and loving and proud. But, in all the times I knew her, I had never seen her cry, never before and never again. My mother sat before me at that table in her yellow dress, her shoulders slouched, tears spilling down her cheeks and onto the top of the linoleum table. She cried and cried and cried. I guess she cried for her children and her home and my father. I guess she cried for herself.

Bob moved in about a month after my father

moved out. He abused each one of us in his own way. Me and my brothers grew up and moved out one by one until he lived alone with my mother, and one day he dropped dead at a campground up near Wilson, New York on Lake Ontario. He lay on his back on a worn dirt road looking past my mother bent over him silhouetted by a radiant blue sky, the life sucked right out of him.

*****

I absently leafed through a church bulletin sitting in that wooden chair waiting for my daughter to come down from her classroom. I decided I would use the word *separation*. It was much gentler than the finality of the word *divorce*. At least that would be a good start. The rest of it I figured I'd better hold back on. We weren't ready yet, and I didn't know if I was sure myself. She arrived at the office in her plaid jumper wearing a shy look of confusion. Her skin was soft ivory and slightly freckled. Her eyes were clear blue. There was no mistaking her as my daughter. I would take her to Anderson's for an ice cream and break it to her gently.

Pedro on the Street Corner

O n this sun-singed afternoon I'm walking down Grant Street on my way to pick up Tony, stopping first at the 7-11 to grab a tall can of Bud, have it put in a brown paper bag high enough to cover it, and amble toward Tony's house. Blinding white sun burns the asphalt gooey soft. The beer slides down my throat cold, foamy, wet. Tony lives in his mother's house. Mom: Angela Lorigo, spreads out like jellied goo in front of a giant whirring fan in her big padded recliner yuk-king it up to an ancient episode of Golden Girls. Legs fat and airy like the Michelin Tire Man. She *is* the Michelin Tire Man in a mismatched house dress, purple goiter on her neck the size of a softball, enormous red face, and her head topped with greasy wisps of frowzy hair. Her fat bare feet are crossed at puffy ankles perched on a stool showing barfy yellow toenails.

I stroll up the porch steps and rap on the screen door, give it a good rat-tat-tat. That show is blasting full volume. Mom turns her goiter my way, "For crying out loud, it's open; he's in the basement."

I move toward her and give a nod, "Hi Mom," I say.

She gives a languid wave, her doughy hand guiding me in the direction of the door to the basement and she does right then let out one hell of a gut-buster when one of those Golden Girls says something wittily snarky.

Downstairs is dim and cool. Tony turned a section of the basement into his bedroom. Lopsided two by fours covered with mismatched paneling are the walls. The room is murky and damp and a persistent stench of mold hangs heavily in the air. A dirty, rust-colored rug of the shag type covers a concrete floor. Piles of sour-smelling clothes lay tossed about. Tony's nestled in a bean bag chair, a remote in his hand, playing one of those video games I don't care much about.

"What's the word, Tony?" I say.

"Did you see Pedro on the corner?" he answers.

"Not while I walked by," I say.

"What are you drinking?"

"Bud."

"Let me have a taste."

"It's gone, Tony; nothing but backwash left."

Tony throws me a disappointed glance, tosses the remote to the side, and puts his arm out. I grab his hand and pull him from the bean bag. Tony stands wiry before me, a head taller, Roman nose, tight lips, hawk's eyes.

"We need to see Pedro," he says. "Word's out that he's looking for us. He's got a job that needs to be done now."

"Pedro's not up front with us, Tony," I say. "He ain't playin' us straight, and he's gonna get us busted."

Tony shoots me a curious look.

"We ain't been busted yet. He keeps an eye out."

"I'm not about to get busted because of Pedro or nobody. I got plans and they don't involve robbin' no houses or breaking into Arab stores and getting wacked by some crazy-ass dune coon," I say. "Them fuckers got guns."

"What're you talkin' 'bout, 'I got plans'?" Tony says, puffing his chest like a Tennessee rooster at a cock fight.

"I'm just sayin' I'm gettin' tired of working for Pedro. We're gonna get burned if we keep relying on him. I'm ready to play it straight before my ass is sittin' in some sorry jail cell with a bunch of east side brothers."

"Damn, baby; you're harsh," Tony says. "Pedro's been takin' care of us a long time. Keepin' *your* pockets filled with cash. You can't forget that shit."

"I'm not forgetting. I'm just tellin' you he ain't pla-yin' us straight no more. His jobs are getting bigger and our asses are gonna get slunk if we get busted. We ain't fifteen anymore. We can get some real time now."

"Well, he's waitin' on us, so we better get movin," Tony says.

*****

We wander down Breckinridge Street past tightly crammed houses, front porches littered with worn mismatched furniture. A summer extension of living rooms packed tightly with screaming kids zigzagging through games of tag, girls with big hooped earrings and short-shorts sucking on long skinny cigarettes, clusters of lithe and muscled young men, tattooed and sleeveless, bunched on porch steps, and flowing into the street. Cicadas hum aggressively under the din of rap blaring from booming car stereos. A police cruiser slices through the street, the shriek of the siren knifing into the scorching afternoon like half melted butter. Heads on the street barely turn.

Tony will do anything for Pedro. Pedro takes care of him. Got him through those stroppy teen years by teaching him how to sniff out easy prey, snag a few bucks, steal bikes, sell a little weed, slide into houses through unlocked windows, rob purses off unsuspecting ladies, learn to strike when some poor sucker is least suspecting, look for unlocked cars, rifle through glove compartments, find this, find that, until it added up to a little something, a little cash in Tony's pocket. A whole lot more in Pedro's. Tony didn't see beyond what chump-change Pedro had to offer. Stupid-ass Tony livin' for the now.

Pedro has boys working for him all through these streets and all these dumb suckers think he's the real deal. Them sayin' shit like, "You seen Pedro on the street corner?" "He lookin' for you, man…got you some work." Big deal, I'm thinkin'.

Pedro does his business in the daytime, on the corner, right out in front of everyone. Everything's word of mouth, no cellphones. Pedro's too smart for that. Nobody's gonna trace his ass.

"Nobody suspects anything during the day," Pedro tells us. "Got to do the business under their nose if you're gonna make it work."

We make it to the corner and Pedro's givin' the goodbye routine to a kid who couldn't be more than thirteen. The parting gesture: handshake, hug, peck on the cheek, slap on the back. The kid swaggers away and we make our move toward Pedro.

Pedro don't move toward us. He don't move toward nobody. We have to approach him like it's a privilege to be on *his* corner, like *he's* some sacred shit, anyway. Tony follows the protocol and gives Pedro a handshake and a hug. I stay a foot or two behind Tony, and Pedro watches me curiously. He is long and lean with one menacing, dark eye that locks onto you. The other is a dead, cloudy, milky mass. It sits lifeless in his stern, chiseled face.

"What's up with you, Johnny Cordero? You got nothin' to say to Pedro?"

"What's up?" I say, holding my stance and letting him know I don't share Tony's admiration. It's a gutsy move to fuck with Pedro.

Pedro tilts his head in my direction holding his good eye on me, looking me over, trying to figure me out, unsure what to say. Pedro smells trouble like a feral cat on the street senses danger lingering in plain sight, ready to strike in an instant. Pedro's been living on these streets all his life; been runnin' the corner about five years. He knows the deal.

"I got a special job for my two special boys," he says, pokin' that evil eye in my direction. "Easy money. I know this old lady who lives in one of those big houses on West Ferry. She's got a lot of jewelry stashed in there. Lives by herself, except she's got housekeeper who leaves every day at six o'clock. *Mi madre* knows the housekeeper, her name is Juana, and the two of them talk when she comes over for a visit sometimes. Anyway, it's a clean job.

After Juana leaves, the old lady goes into the living room and has her supper in the front of the house and watches the six o'clock news. She's half deaf so she turns that television up full loud; old bitty can't hear nothin' but that TV blarin'. I hear she's got plenty of jewelry in that house and you boys can hit the place from the back window."

"When you want us to do this?" Tony asks.

"Man, you can do that shit tomorrow," Pedro says. "This old bag works like clockwork. When Juana leaves it's a guarantee the old ladies in the front room and that shit's sittin' pretty in the back."

"How do you know she doesn't have and alarm?" I say.

"Man, that's the best part. Old Juana slips up and tells *mi madre* that alarm don't get turned on till she's ready to sleep. I hear them talkin' that shit when Juana stops by. It's an easy job Johnny Cordero, and like I say, I'm givin' it to my two special boys."

"You sure about this?" Tony says.

"Hell yeah," Pedro answers. "You borrow your old lady's car and wait a few houses down. Johnny Cordero, you're a skinny fuck; you slide in through that window and score that shit. Shouldn't take you but five minutes."

Pedro musters up a wry smile revealing tiny brown teeth under a flimsy mustache. His milky eye tilted my way. He's one ugly looking cat.

*****

Angela Lorigo sprawls in front of the TV watching the news and eating a plate of fried chicken that sits on one of those metal folding tables made just for that. This one's black with a bunch of red roses painted on it. She's digging into the chicken pretty good, grease glistens on her fingers and around her lips. She's got a two liter of Mountain Dew, and is pouring it into a big plastic glass. Taking a good long swig, washin' the chicken down.

"Ma, let me use your car," Tony says.

"You can take it," she says, between mouthfuls. "Just pick me up a six-pack at the 7-Eleven while you're out."

*****

Tony glides the car down Grant Street making an illegal left onto West Ferry.

"Are you kidding me?" I say. "You want to get busted before we even get there?"

"Relax; I do this shit all the time. There ain't never no one here."

"Shit, I see that big-assed bald cop pullin' people over all the time," I say. "He sits here waitin' on people to make that turn."

We cruise slowly down West Ferry past Rotundo's Dry Cleaning and La Nova's Pizzeria, crawling past a crammed row of worn, lopsided houses. The paint is washed dull from searing summers and frozen winters. Nigerian transplants in long, bright, dazzling dresses fill the sidewalk and front porches, their skin deep purple-black. Tony glides the car through the roundabout on Richmond Avenue and continues slowly toward Elmwood Ave.

With the crossing of a street, we've entered into another world entirely. An abundance of lush trees with closely manicured lawns are spread before us. They're all big-ass houses with plenty of space between them. Some real rich bastards live in this neighborhood. The old lady lives in a gigantic house painted green with beige trim. The paint is glossy and glistens in the afternoon sun. Tony cruises past the house and we get our plan straight.

"Let's swing on back and I'm gonna park right out front," Tony says. "There shouldn't be no problems. I'll give you ten minutes before I have to pull out."

I have a canvas grocery sack hiding under my shirt. Once I'm inside, I'll grab as much shit as I can and fly right on outta there and back into Tony's car. Looks easy enough.

Tony circles the block and slowly pulls the car in front of the house leaving the motor running. A long, narrow driveway leads to a garage in back. There is nobody in sight. The sky is clear and the sun floats high above. I have on a blue cap with a Buffalo Bills logo. I pull it down slightly, step from the car, and move down the driveway toward the back of the house, knowing this is the last time I do any more jobs for Pedro.

"Remember," Tony says, right before I make my move, "you only got ten minutes before I split."

There is no one in the back of the house and it is very quiet. The back bedroom window is open about a foot or so, only a screen separates the bedroom from the outside. I pull out my blade, slicing carefully and evenly along the bottom of the screen so I can glide my fingers on the inside and catch the latches. Pedro's right, the TV *is* blarin'. The weatherman's enthusiastically sayin' something about what a sweltering week it's been. I reach the latches, push them inward and gently lift the screen, stretching my arms as high as they'll go. The window is about neck high. I wrap my hands on the ledge and pull myself upward, sticking my head in and using my shoulders and back to press against the screen and lift it some more so I can wiggle my way in. I get about half way in and feel a pair of hands pressing on my shoulders and yanking me forward, twisting me, and slamming me onto my back and onto a hardwood floor. The barrel of a pistol is pressed firmly against my forehead and a stocky man with thick black hair and dark framed glasses is standing over me.

"So, this is the trash Pedro sends my way," he says, in a voice thick and hazy.

'Fucking Pedro; he burned me,' I'm thinkin' to myself.

By now Tony's split from our parking spot and I am sitting in a chair in the living room with my hands twisting nervously on my lap and a pistol pointed in my direction.

The stocky man is a snappy dresser: blue soft-leather loafers, sockless, with white linen pants and a matching linen shirt opened at the chest showing a thick gold chain around his neck. A big diamond ring on his little finger and a gold bracelet that I'm thinkin' is probably 18 carat. I can tell he's the real deal. He's got cash and strength oozes from him. He ain't no chump like Pedro. He eyeballs me and I wait.

"Pedro told me you'd be paying me a visit," he says, turning down the TV, "and baby, you showed up right on time."

"Where's the old lady?" I say, wondering what this

guy's getting ready to do to me.

"See, that's the kind of trash you are," he says, "trying to steal from an old lady. Well, there is no old lady living here. I live here and I don't like Pedro's puke fucking with this neighborhood."

"I ain't no puke and this was gonna be my last job," I tell the stocky man, and realize how ridiculous that sounds.

He looks me over like he's trying to figure out how he's gonna do me in. I'm wondering, is he gonna kill me with that gun or are we waiting for some thugs to come over and hand me a beating? Toss me around, break some bones, maybe.

"You hungry?" he asks.

"What?"

"Let's go get something to eat," he says.

This guy's got a sweet white Cadillac, 'bout an early seventies model I'm guessing. Chrome bumpers, bright red leather interior. Got a CD player rigged in playing some smooth voiced cat singin' something about *fly me to the moon*.

We cruise down Delaware Avenue, through the S-curves and make a right on Nottingham Road passing by Delaware Park on the right and a row of Tudor houses on the left. The man makes a left turn onto Meadow

Drive, cruises past a couple of houses that look like castles, and pulls the Cadillac into a long driveway with a big stone house nestled in the back. A couple of sweet BMW's and a few Mercedes Benz's are parked here too.

The guy gets out of the Caddy and we walk up a fancy curved sidewalk to the front of the house. The man presses a button next to the door. A series of chimes climbs and echoes from inside and a moment later an old lady opens the door and appears before us in a large foyer with a warm smile. She's a little thing, slightly stooped, with friendly eyes and a tiny head of soft blue-gray hair.

"What takes you so long, Vinny? Everybody's already eating."

"I got a little tied up, Ma," he says.

"What, you bring a friend?" she says, looking at me.

"Yeah, this is…what's your name, kid?"

"Johnny Cordero," I say.

"Johnny Cordero; he's gonna join us."

"That's nice," she says. "Where did you find this Johnny Cordero?"

"He stopped by for a visit and I thought he might like to taste your sauce."

"That's nice," she says again. "Come, everybody's inside."

The little lady leads us down a wide hallway past smooth statues of naked women and big plants in huge pots to a dining room that's 'bout as big as my whole apartment. The table is filled with a basket of bread, a big bowl of spaghetti, another of sausage and meatballs, and a huge bowl filled with salad with tomatoes and cucumbers.

Six men sit hunched around the table filling their mouths with the spaghetti and carrying on a conversation in low murmurs. Bottles of red wine are scattered about the table and the men drink it from short juice glasses. They raise their heads in our direction when we walk in and look me up and down pretty good. The old lady goes back to her seat and Vinny motions for me to take an empty seat next to him. The food comes our way and everyone continues digging in.

One of the guys looks at Vinny, "So, whose this punk you brought with you, Vinny?"

"This kid had the balls to climb into my window," Vinny says. "Thought he was gonna rob an old lady of her jewelry. A regular cat burglar."

"Punk needs to learn a lesson," another says, between mouthfuls of spaghetti.

"Pedro set him up," Vinny says. "Gave the kid a bullshit story about a sure thing."

"No such thing as a *sure* thing," another says.

"Pedro, that little spic that stands on the corner?" another says.

"That's the one," Vinny says.

"Why you want to steal from an old woman?" the old lady says, looking at me. "What's the matter with you?"

These guys are too calm. They're gonna take their time and casually finish up their spaghetti and wine and they're gonna take me in some back room and kick my ass square up. They're just playin' with me.

"Pedro's got a bunch of these punks doing jobs for him and tearing up the neighborhood we grew up in," another says.

A wiry guy with bulging eyes and an Adam's apple that floats up and down his neck looks at me like I'm just another piece of common street shit.

"Where do you live?" he asks.

"On 15th Street near Hampshire," I say.

"See that's the problem," he says. "All you punks are living in our old neighborhood and turning it into a shit-hole, and a scumbag like that Pedro who does his business like a little kid on the street corner is making all the money while you stupid asses are getting popped."

"Pedro set you up," Vinny said looking at me.

"Only reason Pedro would set someone up is if he thinks you aren't loyal to him anymore, so he wants to see your ass taken out. He figures we'd beat you so bad you wouldn't even want to live anymore."

"I say the punk still needs a lesson," the one who said it earlier says, looking at me.

Vinny reaches under the table and pulls out a sack and throws in on the table in front of me.

"This is your lucky day, Johnny Cordero," he says to me.

Inside the sack is an assortment of jewelry, rings, bracelets, necklaces.

"It's all cheap shit," Vinny says, and leans into me. "I want you to give this to Pedro. When that slimy fuck is standing on the street corner, I want you to walk on up and hand him this bag and you tell him you scored big.

"You're not kidding," another says, looking like he wants to tear into a piece of me. "Today is your lucky day."

*****

The fiery sun stabs outrageously onto the street. Pedro's standing on the street corner watching me walk towards him. He looks over my shoulder like he's searching for someone to pop up behind me. He tilts his head and locks his good eye on me; the dead milky one hangs lost on his confused face. He looks at my hand holding the sack.

"You were right, man," I say, handing the sack over to him. "Got me a nice score at that old lady's house. You look this over and let me know my cut."

Pedro leans into me. He knows the score.

"You gonna die for this," he says.

"I ain't gonna die," I say. "Not for you, not for anything. Shit, I got luck on my side!"

COMING HOME

T he plane touched down at the Buffalo airport right after my fifth vodka and orange juice. I had not been home in two years and I had no real desire to come home now, but it *was* my mother's funeral and I was in deep enough trouble with the family to think of an excuse to miss it. I could have thought of a bunch of excuses not to come, some not too far off like I was broke and couldn't afford taking off work and spending cash I didn't have. Money flows when I'm loose. It always has. I suppose I could have faked an injury or a sickness or I could have told my family that my wife was sick with some far-fetched threatening illness, but they wouldn't care much about that, that's for sure.

The trip came at the worst time. I had to borrow a couple of hundred from my wife's stash. She handed it over with a reluctant frown.

"Don't go wild," she said dropping me off at the airport in Denver, "and tell your family to go fuck themselves."

"I'll do that," I said, kissing her good-bye.

My wife Bonnie is an artist. Sometimes she sells her paintings for a pretty good buck, but it's not very consistent and we're not raking in the dough. We're in a transition time she says. I'm not doing much better studying Law during the day and working as a waiter in the evenings. I don't have time to shit, really.

The last time we were both in Buffalo things got pretty screwed up. We were home because my mother had tried her eighth suicide and we thought this one might have put her over the edge. She took a ton of valium and washed them down with about a half bottle of Old Grand-Dad. I never saw my mother drink a drop, so she must have been pretty determined this time. My brother John found her sprawled face up and passed out naked on her bed. He heaved her onto his shoulders, threw her in his van, and carried her limp naked body around his shoulders through the front doors of Sister's Hospital where they plopped her onto a rolling bed and sped her into Emergency. They pumped her stomach, downed glass after glass of water into her, and gave her some drugs to counter the valium. She woke later in a guarded hospital room.

"I need to live in a looney house," she said, looking into my dad with dead eyes.

We were all upset. We did what the Irish do; we drank too much. My family went out that night and ended up at Checker's drinking shots and beers. Later in the night my dad grabbed a piece of Bonnie's ass and she smacked him in the face telling him it was no wonder his wife wanted to kill herself. That got everyone crazy and out of hand. My sisters said Bonnie was a cock tease. Bonnie said, "The next time that fucker touches me I'm gonna cut his balls off." It got real stupid and real ugly. We left the bar, went to my dad's house, got our stuff, and split to my friend's house for the rest of the night. We flew back to Denver the next morning and haven't seen one another since.

*****

My sister Maureen met me at the airport. I hadn't seen her since the incident a couple of years ago. She dropped some pounds and she looked pale and tired. Dull dark circles, like charcoal half-moons, hung under her eyes. Maureen mustered up a smile and gave me an awkward obligatory hug.

"Welcome home," she said.

We drove down the Kensington Expressway toward the city. It was hot and the sticky-wet air clung to me. I had forgotten about the humidity around here. Denver is dry, sometimes oven-dry. I was glad it was summer, though. I didn't think I could take another Buffalo winter.

"Look, there are a lot of people at the house," Maureen said. "Everybody's pretty upset about this, no one saw it coming."

"Christ, she's tried it bunch of times."

"No one thought she'd actually get it done, though," she said. "Anyway, about the last time you were here, just let that slide."

"Dad was out of line," I said.

"He's always out of line; he's a stubborn prick and he can be a real piece of shit, but this has got him really upset. I didn't think he'd take it so hard."

"How's Donald?" I asked.

"He's another piece of shit; we're getting a divorce."

"What?"

"I don't love him, he can't hold a job, and he's a bore."

"Just like that?"

"I've given him time; he sells insurance for Geico for god sakes. He's had one job after another; he's not even *trying* to help out."

"That's too bad," I said.

"Shit happens. Look, he's at the house, so don't say anything to him about it, okay?"

That's my sister, soft as steel assistant district attorney. It's either this or that, right or wrong, yes or no. Donald never had a chance with her.

"You know, Mom couldn't have done this at a worse time," she said. "I've got cases coming out the wazoo. She really picked a fine time."

We drove onto Tillinghast Place to our house. It stood gigantic and white with black shutters adorning each window. I had lived there all of my life until moving to Denver. Maureen pulled into the driveway and turned in my direction.

"Let's go; be nice," she said.

*****

We walked to the back of the house and entered the kitchen door. My brother John was in the kitchen with a beer in one hand and a sandwich, spilling over with ham and cheese, in the other. He wore a pair of bone-white kakis, a blue and white striped oxford shirt, and round tortoise shell glasses. His hair was thick, wild, and sun-bleached. John never stops, he moves at a continuously frantic pace.

"Hey, how are you Matty," he said, wrapping his arm around my neck and pulling me to him. "You look good."

I am a few inches shorter than John and he's got a good fifty pounds on me, a slight gut, but otherwise he's a pretty solid guy. He looked good.

"How 'bout one of those beers?" I asked.

"Sure thing," he said, running to the refrigerator and pulling out a Molson Canadian. He twisted the lid off and handed it to me.

"Well, its official, when I've got one on these in my hand, I'm home."

We tapped our bottles together and I took a long swallow.

"She actually did it this time," he said, taking a mouthful of sandwich. "She actually fuckin' did it."

"It's hard to believe," I said.

"We'll, I guess we got a party out of it," John said.

"Whose here? I asked.

"Everyone, you're the last to arrive. Come on; let's go into the other room."

We moved from the kitchen, through French doors that led into the dining room. A big center staircase separated the dining room from the living room. The rooms were bursting with groups of people, some I knew, and some I'd never seen before. Cousins, friends, neighbors were scattered about, some sitting, some standing, all clustered and chatting with drinks in hand and plates

of food cradled on their laps. Jokes spat out in rapid
fire. You would have thought you were at a Friday night
birthday bash rather than a group of people coming to
comfort one another and mourn the loss of my mother.
The dining room table was loaded with trays of cold cuts,
cheeses, salads, chips, pretzels, and baskets of bread. A
table in the corner held bottles of booze and mixers. The
guests were liberally helping themselves. Adorned on the
wall and moving up the staircase hung years and years of
family portraits. The earliest ones show only my mother
and father. The first being a picture when they are very
young sitting on a blanket at Crystal Beach and smiling
at the camera. The second one shows the two of them
standing in front of St. Mark Church on their wedding
day. My father is wearing a white tuxedo jacket with
black pants and a black bow tie and my mother is in a
long lace wedding dress with a ruffle train flowing before
her. They are young and their eyes are bright and their
smiles are comfortable. Gradually, one by one, each one
of my brothers and sisters and finally me are included
in the portraits with my mother looking more and more
detached in every photo.

John left me and bolted toward some group in the
corner. I searched the room and saw Maureen, presumably, firing off a string of brash instructions to her

husband. He looked past her, lifted his glass and nodded toward me, a meek look frustration on his face. I did not see my father anywhere. My brother Dan was sitting in a chair focused on a tall drink in his hand. When he saw me he casually waved me over.

"Matthew," he said, standing up and giving me a hug. "How the hell are you?"

"Not bad, I guess," I said.

"Can you believe she did it?" he said. "What a bitch."

"No, I can't, really," I said. "It's hard to believe that she'd actually go through with it. I don't think it's really sunk in yet."

"Do you want to do a shot?"

"I don't know; it's still a little early."

"Come on," he said, leading me over to the make-shift bar and pouring two Jamesons. "To our beloved mother Mary O'Brian, one fucked up lady."

Dan knocked back the shot, shuddered, and looked at me.

"Well, drink up," he said.

I took the shot letting it slide down my throat clenching my teeth afterwards.

"I better not do too many of these," I said.

My brother leaned into me, his big square head

inches from face. "You know, Matt, I just want you to know mom was going to do this at some point. Nothing was going to stop her, just a matter of time. It had nothing to do with us. I want you to know that."

"Of course," I said, but I began to think it had everything to do with us. I was beginning to realize it was us that kept her from everything she ever wanted.

*****

One of Dan's disheveled boys, rushed up and tugged his father's arm pulling him away. I stood alone again momentarily lost in the echo of the crowded room. My beer was getting empty and I took the last swallow figuring something stronger might do the trick. I moved toward the booze table and poured myself a stiff whiskey and ginger. I didn't see my dad anywhere. I was about to walk up the stairs to see if he was in his bedroom when my sister Nora intercepted me.

"Little brother," she said, standing before me with a glass of white wine in each hand.

"Hey, Nora," I said.

"Give me a kissy on the cheek," she said. "My hands are full."

We kissed each other's cheeks. She took a step back to tell me how good I looked. Nora looked good too, maybe the best of all of us. Her hair was different than I'd seen it before, long and straight with bangs cut just before her eyebrows, and dyed brick red. It had always been a dull brown, but this new look really perked her up. She wore a simple, short white summer dress and had on a pair of red cowboy boots. Her lips looked more painted and poutier than I remember.

"How's Nashville?" I asked.

"It's great. I'm singing in some of the best clubs, and getting a gig singing some back-up on John Prine's next record. I'm meeting important people, Matty. Good musicians, and pretty soon I'm going to cut my own record at one of the studios down there.

"That's great," I said.

"You should come down, bring Bonnie with you."

"Sure, where's Dad?"

"I don't know; I haven't seen him."

"How come all these people are here and nobody knows where Dad is? Has anybody seen him?"

"Hell if I know. I'm sure he's around somewhere," she said, and downed one of her white wines. "I guess he's upset or something."

"I'm going upstairs," I said.

"Give me another kissy," she said, raising her chin and puckering her lips.

I laid one on her cheek and walked up the long stairway. It was much quieter upstairs. The bedroom doors were open and I looked into my room, the one John and I shared for so many years. Bunk beds, baseball and football trophy's, pictures of us as kids, a typical room, a holding place for untainted youth, a safe haven before all of the bullshit. The room at the end of the hall belonged to my parents. A room they shared for more than forty years.

The door was slightly open and it was very quiet inside. I knocked lightly.

"It's open," my Father said.

"Hey, Dad." I said. "I was *wondering* where you were."

I looked at my father's massive back hunched over his desk writing on some stationary. He turned in my direction and gave me a somber look of a man tired and confused.

"Matthew," he said, focusing on me as if he had just woken from a deep sleep. "You made it."

My dad is a big man with a thick head of grey-black streaked hair that sits tousled on a wide face with powerful brown eyes. He wears wire rimmed glasses that give him the look of an intellectual rugby player.

"It didn't take long," I said. "I got a flight right

away."

"I'm glad you made it; I'm happy you're here."

I moved closer to him and bent down to give him a hug. I felt his huge hand patting my back, like some scene from a movie, and realized I couldn't remember ever hugging my father. He looked at me with worn glassy eyes.

"You know, I did grab Bonnie's ass that night," he said. "I grabbed it real good."

"We were all drunk. We don't need to bring that up now, Dad."

"Bonnie was right," he said. "Anyone married to me would probably have to kill themselves. I was an impossible bastard."

"You're upset. Everything's going to feel strange for a while until things settle down."

"Well, I'm just saying I was a too hard on her that night. We all were, and I'm sorry it happened like that. I want to tell her I'm sorry."

"Thanks," I said, looking at him unsure what to do next.

"It's a powerful person that can hate someone enough to kill themselves," my dad said. "That's something you have to really dig deep to do."

"What are you talking about, Dad?"

"Not what, who. I'm talking about your mother. I'm talking about her despising me enough to take her own life. I'm talking about her punishing me for the things I've done. I should have apologized to her long ago. I had opportunities, but I never did. I was so god-damned stubborn that I couldn't muster up the decency to apologize to my own wife for my behavior."

"Mom had problems, deeper than *we* or *she* could handle," I said.

"That's where you're wrong, Matt. We should have made it easier for her. I asked her once if we were worth it – we as a family – I asked her if our family was worth it. She gave me a blank stare and walked from the room. I remember that well."

"Why aren't you downstairs, Dad?" I said. "Why aren't you downstairs with everyone? They're all going to be gone in a couple of days and you'll have plenty of time to be alone in this house."

"I'm writing an apology to your mother; it's going right with her in the grave. I have to do this before I can move," he said, turning back into his writing table.

Once again I looked at his massive shoulders and thick head of grey-black hair. He leaned into the writing table staring at his paper, momentarily lost in an emotional void.

"I guess I'll go downstairs," I said. "Hurry up, will you?"

My dad tapped his pen a couple of times, turned in my direction, and looked me over.

"Matt, you want to go down to Checker's for a beer?" he said.

"What?"

He picked up the apology, or what was written, folded it neatly and put it in his front shirt pocket.

"Sure, let's go out the back door and get out of here for a while," he said. "We'll be back. Let's go – you and me for a beer."

*****

Checker's was quiet. Sully, the bar tender, casually hosted some of the late afternoon old-timers slouched on barstools, silently drinking beer from bottles and knocking back an occasional shot of cheap whiskey. Sully had the television tuned to golf and some of the old-timers commented, to themselves, on various putts, chip shots and fairway drives. Sully wiped the bar before us and threw down two cocktail napkins. He was slender, in his mid-thirties, with a mop of soft-curly black hair and a baby face. He leaned into the bar and greeted us with pale-blue eyes.

"Sorry for your loss," Sully said to both of us. "She was a fine woman."

"She was at that, Sully," my father said.

Sully poured two pints of Guinness and placed a shot of Jameson before each of us.

"These are on me," he said, and we three toasted my mother's journey and drank the shots. Sully poured us two more pints.

I wondered if anyone back at the house knew we had left. I had to believe the party was picking up steam, getting louder; my brother's probably beckoning the group and toasting to the tortured soul of their departed mother; stories of remembrance drooling from the mouths of teary-eyed family and friends. They would honor her soul late into the evening.

My father settled comfortably on his barstool. The early-evening crowd was filing in. Friends from the neighborhood strolled in for a quick beer before going home to their families for dinner. They greeted my father, grasping his hand, patting his back, and shaking their heads in disbelief at his tragic loss. Each nodded toward Sully to get us a drink. Tiny upside-down shot glasses stood before us, all good for another round. Sully kept pouring and me and my dad kept drinking. I figured the old man couldn't be any more relaxed than he was right now.

My dad pulled out the apology letter from his shirt pocket and looked it over. He laid it before him on the bar, smoothing out the creases with his big hands. I could see a full page of writing before me, thin black ink scribbled delicately on paper in his unmistakable handwriting. For a big man, my father's handwriting had an effeminate quality, curly long tapered letters and circular dotted I's. The letter remained on the bar unnoticed. Sully placed more beers and shot glasses before us, some of the glasses dropped right onto the letter itself.

As the evening wore on, my father drank more and more and insisted that Sully "fire up the jukebox" and play *Dirty Old Town* by The Pogues.

"Turn it up, Sully," my father insisted, and Shane McGowan crooned and my dad cried.

After another hour or so, I was finally able to convince my dad that we needed to get back home.

"We have a house full of people," I reminded him.

"Let's get outta here, Matty," my father said, and he swayed slowly out from the bar receiving a series of hugs, good luck's and goodbye's. We exited the big wooden door onto Hertel Avenue with the apology letter stuck to the bar, the ink smeared wet and runny under a pile of empty glasses.

The Pier

We walked down the pier with our fishing poles in our hands. Michael carried a bucket of live herring for bait. He was hoping to catch something big. By the time we reached the end, the water was deep. Spread before us spanned the eternal blue-green sea. In the distance, an infinite spectacle of white caps broke, but they were very small. Behind us, on the shore, stretched endless white and pink buildings surrounded by palm trees. Some stood tall and thin; others were thick and low to the ground.

We positioned ourselves at the far right corner of the pier. The sun hovered directly above, locking firmly onto a cloudless sky. Michael decided to cast into the deeper water. He pulled a herring from the bucket, securing its head firmly on the hook. Its silver back glistened in the sunlight. With fine precision he held the pole behind him, and with a long arching motion he sent the rig flying far into the sea. When the rig plopped into the water he let it settle, and then cocked the reel so no more line would escape.

He trolled gently back towards the pier. The line was taut and if he got a hit the pole would bend quickly with great force. He knew he might have luck landing a grouper or a snapper. There were plenty of them in these waters. And, he knew he could reel in kingfish, cobia, tuna, amberjack, Spanish mackerel, dolphin, shark, barracuda, mahi-mahi, tarpon, or any number of exotic fish.

This excited him. He was used to trolling for northern pike or muskie along the Niagara River or going out into Lake Erie for perch and small-mouth bass. Great fishing, but nothing compared to what we could pull out here. The Gulf was unpredictable; anything could bite.

I pulled out a herring and placed it in the palm of my hand, its shiny white belly glistening before me. I slid the hook firmly in front of the anal fin and down through its body. Then, I cast my pole letting the rig pop into the water and find its way down while cocking the reel and letting line drift and tighten from the weight of the sinker and the current. I did not reel in. I chose instead to sit back and watch those around us pulling in their catches. There was a slight warm breeze, and the simple fragrance of clean fresh salty air was lazily pleasing.

To our left a shirtless, sun-bleached, leather-faced man stood hunched over the railing dropping his line beneath him and pointing his pole directly towards the water. He wore a straw hat with a wide brim. He fished quietly and earnestly, methodically swaying his pole back and forth in a hypnotic rhythmic motion. Fishing a little further down stood a man burned terribly by the sun, presumably a Northerner, probably on vacation or down to visit an elderly parent. I wasn't sure, but I figured it had to be something like that. And so it was, we were on this wonderful pier that stretched far into the Gulf, quietly and patiently waiting to land a big fish. To have those around us clamor with excitement when one of us pulled in a beauty.

Sitting on a bench with my legs up on the railing, I could hear the Northerner strike up a conversation with the old man wearing the straw hat.

"Boy, I sure would love to hook into a large tarpon," the Northerner said with enthusiasm.

"No you wouldn't," the old man quickly replied.

"Why not?"

"Because if you hook into a two-hundred pound tarpon standing on this pier, he's gonna hurt you."

"I'll bet it'll take a couple of hours just to reel him in," he said, trying to sound as if he knew something about tarpon.

"No it wouldn't," the old man said. "But, I guarantee you that bastard will hurt you. You hook a two-hundred pound fish that size, he's three times his weight in the water. That bastard is strong and mad. With no leverage, he'll break your back."

"Well, hell, if you ever brought him in there would be plenty of good meat on 'em."

"They're sport fish," the old man said. "Meat's no good; too many bones."

The Northerner dropped his rig into the water trying, in poor imitation, to mimic the smooth technique of the old man. The sun was high in the sky. It reflected in the water like many bright stars on a clear night. Far out on the horizon a ship headed south. Scattered among us brown pelicans sat nestled on the railing or near the edge of the pier lazily waiting for hand-outs. It was quiet and each of us was lost in our own thoughts enjoying the tranquility of the sizzling Florida afternoon. Michael was deep in his own rhythmic trance, maneuvering and pulling in his line slowly and deliberately.

Very close to the pier I saw the fin of a porpoise then nothing. A moment later I saw the whole animal black and shiny from the sun and water. It rose up and cut back down in a series of poetic movements. The Northerner's eyes excitedly followed the movement as well.

"Nice dolphin," he said to the old man.

"That's not a dolphin," the old man snapped.

"Like hell it isn't."

"Like hell nothing. That's a porpoise not a dolphin; there's a difference, a tremendous difference."

"Well, I thought they were the same; a dolphin is the same as a porpoise and a porpoise is the same as a dolphin. They're the same thing."

"Well, they're not," the old man insisted.

"Well, I thought they were."

"Well, they're not."

I couldn't help but thinking what a bastard that old man was. He wouldn't give that Northerner a break.

We had been fishing for about an hour and the two men quit talking. It was a slow day and none of us had much luck. It was very hot. I never got a bite. Michael reeled in a couple of small catfish and the Northerner pulled in one catfish and a couple mullet. The mullets were olive green with blue tints on their backs. Their silvery sides blended into a creamy white belly. He threw the catfish back and tossed the mullets to the tramping pelicans. They swallowed them whole quickly raising their heads to the sky and letting the fish slide down their throats. This awakened the seagulls who circled the pelicans sending out high piercing shrieks in anticipation of a dropped morsel.

The old man was displeased with the actions of the Northerner.

"You know when you give one pelican a fish, you rile up the whole of them and the gulls too…causes too much commotion. Y'all should leave things as they are."

"Sorry," the Northerner said.

"Things are different here. It's a different kind of fishin' than up North. You fish up there?" the old man asked.

"Yep, mostly trout in the streams. I use light hooks usually number sixes. Catch 'em best with salmon eggs."

"Well I reckon you can at least snag a trout."

"What?"

"Nothin'."

"Do you enjoy eating snook?" the Northerner asked.

"They're the tastiest fish to eat down here. Most Northerners don't know that, sweet as hell."

"I should try it sometime."

The old man stared coldly at the Northerner with dull, cruel shark eyes. He crouched into a pugnacious stance.

"Don't talk to me you damn-bastard!"

"Ease up," the Northerner said.

"Your pale skin will burn and blister in this sun!"

Just then the Northerner felt a tremendous jerk on his pole, then another, then a very powerful tug. He raised his arms and held both hands tightly on the foam handle. The pole arched downward and he was losing it.

"Give him some line!" the old man shouted.

The line spun out whirring and drawing the attention those fishing nearby. The pelicans lifted their heads with eager anticipation. The gulls hovered excitedly overhead. The fish bolted towards the bottom. Then he came up fast and broke the surface. I could see his long lean body, his translucent green dorsal fin. A thin black stripe ran across his body from head to tail. He crashed down and again headed for deep water.

"You got a snook!" the old man yelled. "Pound for pound he's the toughest fish to catch! Bring him in you pale bastard! He's thirty pounds I'm sure!"

The Northerner did all he could to work with the fish and reel him in. He let up giving the fish line and began reeling in. He could feel its strength and tried to keep control of the fish cutting sharply in the water. The snook was trying, with all his power, to rid himself of the hook. Fifteen minutes passed and the snook was tired and almost up.

"Bring him in easy you Northern ass, you pale

scum."

The fish was now only a few yards below us on the surface. He was tired and being led easily to the pier. Once the fish was directly underneath the Northerner lifted the fish half way out of the water. A crowd had gathered and was impressed by the size of the snook. In an instant, the fish turned slightly and the hook slipped easily from his mouth freeing him back into the deep water.

"You worthless Northern scum!" the old man screamed. "You snotty bastard! I hate you, you bastard!"

The Northerner stepped backwards and avoided a punch that would have hit hard. At that moment, from out of nowhere, a well muscled man reached up and under the old man, stilling him with a half-nelson and reminding him his behavior needed to change.

"Come on now," the muscled man said. "Fishing is over for today."

"How'd I do?" the old man asked, suddenly speaking in the tone of a little boy.

"Pretty good, Jerry. You did all right."

"Did I catch many fish?"

"You caught a whole bunch, Jerry," the muscled man said, letting go of the old man and helping him gather his fishing tackle. "I threw them back for you. You know we like to leave them here."

"Were they big?"

"Very."

"Good."

"I'm sorry," the muscled man said to the Northerner. "I was watching. He usually doesn't get like that, at least not in a long time. He's pretty cracked up. We let him out once in a while to get some fresh air and see if he remembers."

"That's okay."

"I probably shouldn't have let it go that far."

"Again, it's okay."

The old man neatly packed his tackle and stood calmly waiting for instructions from the muscled man.

A pelican lifted his head to the sky, fluttered his wings, and settled back into slumber.

"Take care," the muscled man said.

"You too," replied the Northerner.

"It was nice meeting you," the old man said to the Northerner. "You're a very nice gentleman. It was a pleasure. Goodbye."

The old man and the well muscled man walked down the pier towards the shore. The old man focused ahead while the other craned his neck to notice the catches brought in by other fishermen. The Northerner looked at me, shook his head, then cast a short distance letting his line drop until it became taut and slowly reeled it back in. He caught a few more mullet and a few more catfish using this strategy. He threw them all back.

The sun was setting behind the shore now and the water had turned a deeper blue. Michael and I grabbed our tackle and packed it neatly. Michael dumped the fish from the bait bucket into the water. We walked to the shore passing underneath a big sign that read: *The gods do not subtract from the allotted span of men's lives the hours spent in fishing.*

Mr. Lebrun

Mr. LeBrun paced nervously backstage just before the curtain rose
at the South Side High School's
production of *Annie*. The theatre
was full. It was opening night and all of the normal jitters
were in place. Not only was Mr. LeBrun an outstanding
math teacher at the school, he was the musical director,
and the moments preceding curtain-up always kept him
on edge. One source of comfort for him was that all of
the rehearsals had gone fairly well. The shows they did
for the junior high school and the elementary school
went off without any problems, except the actors didn't
like the fact that the *younger audience* didn't get some of
the adult jokes sprinkled into the play.

Mr. LeBrun wandered about with an effeminate
gait. Beads of perspiration glistened on his forehead. He
was a large man with big hands, huge feet, and hunched
shoulders. His huge belly sagged like jellied slop over
his belt buckle. His feet were perpetually sore, so he
wore those soft, black Dr. Scholl's shoes to help him get

through long days of teaching and rehearsals. Mr. LeBrun had a smooth, pink complexion and lively brown eyes. His chin was long and flat with a cleft right in the center and he looked a bit like a young Bob Hope, except as I mentioned earlier, he had quite a large frame.

Mr. LeBrun moved deliberately about the backstage area anxiously checking that everything was in order. He made sure the prop mistress had each prop numbered and correctly placed on the tables in the wings of the stage. Mr. LeBrun caught the eye of the fat boy, wearing an un-tucked white shirt, running the pin rail. He made sure the boy had his script in hand and that he knew precisely when to pull the hand lines to lower the battens that held the different scrims, curtains and scenery drops for scene changes. Mr. LeBrun reminded the boy that scene changes had to be quick and flawless.

"The audience should barely notice," he instructed the boy.

Mr. LeBrun touched base with his wardrobe crew and reminded the two giggling girls of a couple of quick changes they would need to make, especially Annie's costume change before the Christmas scene.

Mr. LeBrun was confident that all of his actors had their lines memorized. They had painstakingly blocked each scene many times, giving him assurance that they knew where to position themselves on the stage. During rehearsals the singers hit their notes and the dancers moved gracefully on cue. Mr. LeBrun was content with all of this and was confident in his band director's ability to get the band to know all of the music. During the dress rehearsals this was evident. The band played brilliantly. His choreographer had done a delightful job with the dance numbers. *Hard Knock Life* was a big number and the little orphans nailed it. He even did a fine job with Daddy Warbucks and Annie dancing gracefully to *I Don't Need Anything But You* which all of the kids figured was going to be a disaster because Robbie, who played Daddy Warbucks, had two left feet. The choreographer figured it would be best if Annie took the lead and to Mr. LeBrun's delight, the two danced about the stage effortlessly. It really was a touching moment on the South Side Stage.

*****

The day after the show, Mr. LeBrun sat in the teacher's lunchroom devouring the same thing he ate every day at lunchtime: A ham sandwich with Swiss cheese and lettuce on white bread, an apple, and a sleeve of Oreo cookies with two pints of milk.

Generally, Mr. LeBrun did not frequent the teacher's lunchroom, preferring rather to have lunch in his own classroom with some of the students involved with the musical, but for a few days after a show, he enjoyed the accolades he received from the excited teaching staff.

He bathed in the delights of the complimentary tidbits of talk swirling excitingly throughout the room complimenting what a great show *Annie* was. Nobody could believe Robbie could sing like that, and they all enthusiastically agreed that the little orphans were just great! Mr. Welgy, the Earth Science teacher, said he wouldn't be surprised if Robbie didn't have a shot at Broadway, and Mrs. Stewart, the Social Studies teacher, added that Jenny Moore, who played Annie, deserved a shot, too. They were both that good, they agreed.

Mr. LeBrun listened to the chatter around him with great appreciation. His ego was up pretty high while sitting in that teacher's cafeteria finishing his Oreo cookies.

*****

Mr. LeBrun lived in a sturdy two-story red brick house a block from the school, with his wife, a gym teacher, who taught at the same high school. Mrs. LeBrun kept their lawn perfectly manicured, and the boxwood shrubs lining underneath the front windows were trimmed and molded to perfection.

Mrs. LeBrun was a short woman with deep dark brown eyes, thick, muscular legs, and a very short haircut. She had square shoulders and did not wear any make-up or jewelry. At work she wore sneakers, shorts, and a white t-shirt. A whistle with a bunch of keys dangled on a long lanyard from her neck. If she had to dress up for any reason, she wore flat shoes, never heels.

The Lebrun's never spoke with one another at work and always somehow had separate schedules. They never shared a free period or a lunch period together. Most people in the school forgot they were actually married.

Together, Mr. LeBrun and his wife had a cordial relationship. They slept in separate bedrooms in their home. Mrs. Lebrun's room was on the first floor directly next to the kitchen and Mr. LeBrun's room was in the back of the house on the second floor looking out over the flower garden.

Every Friday evening they dined together at a restaurant in downtown Buffalo. Usually they went to a local tavern for a Friday night fish fry. Mr. LeBrun drank a chilled glass of white wine with two ice cubes and Mrs. LeBrun would indulge in a bourbon Manhattan, straight up. They took their time with dinner and usually conversed, in quiet demeanors, sparsely, about their week at the school.

Most every Saturday evening Mrs. LeBrun dined with Diane and Mary Alice, two physical education teachers she had gone to high school with. The three of them had remained close friends through the years. They also vacationed together in Europe for four weeks each summer. Last year they went to southern France and Spain.

On Sunday mornings Mr. LeBrun made a large breakfast filling the kitchen with the comforting scent of fresh coffee and scrambled eggs with bacon while Mrs. LeBrun slept soundly in her bedroom. While waiting for his wife to wake, put on her robe and join him in the back parlor, Mr. LeBrun would read the New York Times cover to cover while sipping dark French roast coffee. He spent most of his time reading the Arts section, paying particular attention to the theatre news.

The LeBrun's passed their time on the weekends rather routinely. When the weather was warm and clear they took long wandering drives roaming the area and looking for lawn sales or farmers markets. In the autumn they'd take a slow meandering drive under the golden, burnt orange, and fiery red trees to the Boston Hills and buy a bushel of apples and a gallon of fresh squeezed apple cider. Mrs. LeBrun would use the apples to make pies and homemade applesauce.

But it was in school, during the week, with the kids when Mr. LeBrun was happiest. He could not get enough of seeing them, of being surrounded by them. Their energy, their enthusiasm; he gloated when they entered his space.

Mr. LeBrun was quite popular with the kids. Some came into his classroom during their lunches or study halls to have long, fun bantering conversations with their favorite teacher. They wrote notes on his black-board and on his file cabinets and on pieces on paper that Mr. LeBrun happily and haphazardly stuck onto his classroom walls. When one walked into his classroom anyone could read that *Mr. LeBrun was the best teacher in the world!* Or, *Mr. LeBrun was the coolest!* He was not gruff; he did not raise his voice or give off an air of superiority toward the students. They felt very comfortable with Mr. LeBrun.

It was as if Mr. LeBrun was just an older version of his students. He understood them. He wanted to be with them. In his mind he was one of them.

*****

Mr. LeBrun had a close friend named Mr. Carne who played the piano. He was a music teacher at West High School, a newer and more modern school on the west end of town. Where South was a majestic and traditional massive white-brick building with carved stone pillars under gigantic oak trees, West was a modern sprawling structure made of glass and blue steel. Mr. Carne often helped Mr. LeBrun choose shows based on the difficulty of the music. One year Mr. Carne talked Mr. LeBrun out of having his school perform *West Side Story* explaining that the music was too difficult.

"Who could even sing Maria's parts?" Mr. Carne asked.

The same went for *Jesus Christ Superstar*. "The music is just too hard to do well," he said.

Still, Mr. Carne suggested a number of fine shows that the kids could perform very well. Some of the most memorable shows the two collaborated on included *Kiss Me Kate, The Boyfriend, Godspell* and *Crazy for You.* Mr. LeBrun was particularly fond of *Crazy for You* as it featured the music of the Gershwin's, his favorite composer and lyricist. Mr. Carne played the piano during those shows and the two were quite famous for putting on spectacular theatre at South Side High School.

*****

Each spring Mr. LeBrun and Mr. Carne took a group of students on a three-day trip to New York City to see a Broadway show. It was a big event and all of the actors and stage crew and band members looked forward to the trip. This year, Mr. LeBrun and Mr. Carne scheduled a meeting in early September to go over a list of fundraising opportunities for the students to engage in. It was a costly trip and the more money the students made fundraising, the better.

In the past, students sold candles, oranges and grapefruits, big decorative tins of popcorn, and coupon books. Some years they held Saturday afternoon car washing events and some years they had a big spaghetti dinner in the student cafeteria with a Chinese auction.

This year the group unanimously decided on the spaghetti dinner, thinking they would gain the most profit from it. A basket raffle was decided upon and all students were expected to create a theme basket and bring it to the dinner. Mr. Barone, the Honor Society advisor, offered his students to volunteer their services and help work the dinner. Mr. LeBrun went to the PTA meeting and solicited their support as well. As they did every year, the ladies of the PTA volunteered their services by helping to run the event. Mrs. Marino, who had two students at the school, said her younger brother owned Angelo's Italian Restaurant and Angelo would be happy to donate the spaghetti, salad, and fresh bread. Mrs. Peters volunteered to run a bake sale.

"We could charge fifty cents a dessert," she said.

The spaghetti dinner was a huge success. The mothers from the PTA busily decorated the cafeteria with plastic red and white checkered table clothes and Mr. Jenkins, the night custodian, turned off a few of the big over head lights telling the ladies it gave the room *ambiance.* Mrs. Hayes, who had three students of her own at South Side High School, brought in a bag of battery operated candles and had a couple of Honor Society volunteers place one on each table. Her oldest son, John Hayes, played the bassoon and was going on the trip.

Mrs. Peters positioned two cafeteria tables next to one another and spread a large flowered table cloth over them. She placed trays of baked goods on them and got two kids to sell the desserts. When the doors opened, the cafeteria filled quickly with eager parents and students. Many folks in the community stopped in and ordered spaghetti dinners to go. A whole dinner only cost eight dollars.

In the corner of the cafeteria, a small string ensemble played Vivaldi's *Four Seasons.* The students sat on cafeteria chairs while playing. The girls wore long black dresses and the boys wore black pants with white shirts.

Mr. LeBrun arrived wearing a bright smile and a

short sleeved white shirt. His hairy arms stuck out and beads of perspiration dotted his balding head. He and Mr. Carne purchased a spaghetti dinner and sat at a long table crowded with a jovial group of admiring students. Mr. LeBrun filled himself with voracious mouthfuls of spaghetti and joked with the kids about what a fine bus they were going to take to New York.

"We ain't taking no cheese bus," he chuckled, in a southern black accent amusingly tilting his head to one side. "We goin' high-class." The kids loved it when he broke into that accent. That meant he was having a good time.

The parents looked at Mr. LeBrun as a bit of a celebrity and flocked for their turn to get a word with him. The parents adored him. They agreed that he brought *a bit of Broadway* to the school. After eating a mound of spaghetti, Mr. LeBrun helped himself to a cup of coffee from the big pot next to the dessert table, filling it with plenty of sugar and milk. He sauntered eagerly about the cafeteria chatting with countless parents about past shows and their children who had performed in those shows long ago. Mr. LeBrun enjoyed the attention; it was always a special night for him.

The trip to New York was not scheduled until April. The spaghetti dinner brought in close to five-thousand dollars to pay for the trip. Once the calculations were tallied, the remaining parent cost for each student was around two-hundred dollars. That would cover the bus, the hotel room in Manhattan and the cost of a matinee ticket for *The Phantom of the Opera* at the Majestic Theatre. That money also included a couple of meals at restaurants throughout the city.

*****

It was six-thirty on a dark chilly spring morning when the students boarded the bus in the school parking lot. The trip was scheduled to last from Thursday to Sunday morning.

Before boarding, parents and students assembled in the cafeteria where Mr. LeBrun, Mr. Carne, and two parent chaperones gave students last minute instructions. They assured uneasy parents their children were in good hands. Mr. LeBrun had given the parents his cell number and told them they could call him directly if there was an emergency. He gave each student a seating assignment and told them who would be partnering with whom for the duration of the trip.

The kids hopped eagerly onto the bus excited by the big comfortable adjustable seats. There was plenty of leg room. Televisions played Looney Tunes on the bus, too. Mr. Lebrun settled comfortably in the front seat wearing blue jeans, a white buttoned oxford shirt, a blue sport coat and a black beret tilted on his large head.

Seven hours later the bus pulled up to the Hilton Garden Inn in Times Square. The students tiredly exited the bus and assembled in the lobby of the hotel.

A dark slender man in a navy blue suit greeted Mr. LeBrun. The two spoke briefly, and the man gave Mr. LeBrun a large manila envelope. Inside of the envelope room keys were placed in smaller white envelopes with the room numbers printed on the outside. Mr. LeBrun, Mr. Carne, and the two other chaperones divided the envelopes and gathered their groups accordingly. Each chaperone passed the envelopes to their students and after this brief exchange, the group headed excitedly to their rooms. The chaperones, Mr. Carne, and Mr. LeBrun had their own separate rooms.

The stay in New York was a whirlwind of adventure filled with fun and thrilling things to do. The group moved through the Manhattan streets at a frantic pace touring Ellis Island, The Statue of Liberty, Rockefeller Center, and Radio City Music Hall. They rode the lightning fast elevators and ascended to the observation deck of the Empire State Building looking at the incredible 360-degree view of New York and beyond, and they spent some time roaming through the twisting pathways in Central Park. They had New York style pizza at John's Pizza in the West Village and they enjoyed lunch from a hot dog cart in Midtown. At the Majestic Theatre they took an acting workshop with one of the cast members from *The Phantom of the Opera*, and the highlight of the trip, the show itself, was pure splendor and excitement. When the kids got on the bus and headed back to Buffalo they were exhausted, and filled with a contentment of dreams and possibilities New York and the world had to offer.

*****

It wasn't until about a week later that the rumors began swirling. They floated into the school lightly like the first delicate snowflakes swaying from a deep black sky of a dismal pending storm.

Robbie, the boy who played Daddy Warbucks, had mentioned to a couple of friends while eating in the noisy school cafeteria of a peculiar interaction between himself and Mr. LeBrun while they were in New York.

Robbie let his friends know that Mr. LeBrun had called him to his hotel room to ask advice concerning where the group might eat lunch on that day. Mr. LeBrun sat poised delicately on the edge of his bed and motioned for Robbie to sit next to him. What gave Robbie a peculiar feeling was the length of time Mr. LeBrun rested his hand on Robbie's knee. Mr. LeBrun's heavy fleshy hand trailed slowly up Robbie's thigh until Robbie abruptly stood up and said, "Pizza would be best for the group," and hurriedly left the hotel room. Robbie confessed to his tablemates that he felt uneasy because Mr. LeBrun clearly had a bulge growing in his groin and his face held a weirdly dreamy expression.

Before weeks end, Principal Meer received a number of phone calls from confused parents. Superintendent Freeman phoned Principal Meer explaining he had received phone calls concerning Mr. LeBrun as well. Two days later Superintendent Freeman and Principal Meer summoned Mr. LeBrun from his classroom to Principal Meer's office and confided with him what they had learned. They informed Mr. LeBrun that a phone call to the police had been made and a full investigation would follow.

Mr. LeBrun shifted uncomfortably in a stiff wooden chair before the men. Large beads of perspiration slid down his forehead. He admitted to nothing stating that the story was fabricated and ridiculous. Even so, at the end of the meeting it was agreed that it would be best for Mr. LeBrun to resign immediately from his position as a math teacher at South Side High School. Superintendent Freeman and Principal Meer sealed the deal by shaking, with trepidation, Mr. LeBrun's damp meaty hand. Mr. LeBrun lowered his head and shoulders and muttered, "I've been having some issues lately," and he lumbered woefully from the office and out of the school.

You would have expected this to have blown up all over the school and pierce through the community in an electronically viral shark attack or witch-hunt. But, it was strangely rather lackluster. It was as if the community turned a blind eye on the whole matter, as if nobody wanted to uncover anything that would put a blemish on South Side High School.

Mrs. LeBrun said nothing of the matter openly. She continued to teach her classes without comment until silently retiring at the end of June. It was as if she had vanished. There were no celebratory parties or gatherings for her; she simply dismissed any small attempt at fanfare in her honor. She had just reached thirty years of teaching and had contributed into the retirement system which would bring in a comfortable pension. Mrs. LeBrun would have rather worked for a few more years, but her quiet dignity had been torn from her and she wanted nothing more to do with South Side High School.

On the last day of school she cleaned out her desk

and walked away from South Side for good embarking on an eight week trip to the Austrian and Italian Alps with Diane and Mary Alice.

After leaving Principal Meer's office Mr. LeBrun walked quietly to his home and cancelled his telephone services. He excluded himself from the world and remained cloistered in his home, mostly in his bedroom on the second floor of the house. He read vigorously while lying in his bed eating enormous mounds of food. His existence was fueled and fulfilled by food and literature. He delved into authors he never had time to read before. They required a heavy commitment. You needed to work hard to get through their books; it was an effort. Mr. LeBrun began taking on writers like Moliere, Ibsen, Faulkner, Melville, Descartes, Shakespeare and reading all of their stories.

While Mrs. LeBrun was completing her tenure at South Side High School, and before her trip to the Austrian and Italian Alps, Mr. LeBrun woke each morning at nine o'clock and cooked himself a big breakfast: a six-egg omelet, sausages, bacon, pancakes smothered in butter and maple syrup. He waited uneasily for his to wife leave before he emerged from his room.

Their relationship consisted mainly of avoiding one another. They spoke rarely and about nothing of significance. Mrs. LeBrun felt an empty hollowness toward her husband, feeling no pity or sympathy for him. Mr. LeBrun cooked his morning meal then sat alone at the kitchen table reading the newspaper and looking at the surroundings of his quaint little kitchen. The room was always silent, nothing stirred. An old clock ticked nervously on the wall above the kitchen table.

Life was calm and strangely fulfilling for Mr. LeBrun during this time. He spent his hours alone voraciously eating enormous piles of food, reading insatiably, and avoiding his wife. His girth expanded until his clothing did not fit comfortably any longer. He resorted to wearing a soft cotton bathrobe as his principal garment. When Mrs. LeBrun finally left for her travels, Mr. LeBrun locked the doors, closed all of the curtains in their home, and wandered through the silent rooms naked, resembling a soft-bloated mound of something hideous.

Because Mrs. LeBrun would not be home for quite some time, Mr. LeBrun was able to roam freely throughout the house. He took to smoking cigars, filling the dry air with stale smoke. Showers and baths became more infrequent and Mr. LeBrun released a sour rotten stench. His hair grew into long slippery wisps and his complexion became ruddy with an oily sheen to it. A musty cloud hung in every room. Mr. LeBrun had read all of the books in the house and now spent his days lying naked on his bed, insatiably eating, smoking cigars, and watching one show after another on his perpetually turned on television. Getting downstairs into the kitchen to make meals became more and more difficult so he prepared large quantities of food and lugged them up to his room in a brown paper sack keeping a supply that would last him a couple of days at a time.

Weeks passed. The weather turned hot and sticky. The air was still and heavy with the humidity climbing to a suffocating one hundred percent. Flies buzzed noisily in the stagnant scorching room among putrid bags of garbage. Mr. LeBrun lay perspiring on his grimy brown and yellowed sheets finding it more and more difficult to move. Remnants of cigar ashes dropped here and there on his mattress smearing his filthy sheets with grayish smudges.

*****

Detective Charles Fogarty, Chief of the Arson Squad, spoke to Mrs. LeBrun in his tiny office at the Buffalo Fire Headquarters on Court Street. Fogarty's desk was a large, messy, grey-steel piece with papers stacked and scattered haphazardly about. The air was stale and dry. A picture of him with his wife and two daughters standing in front of Niagara Falls on a boat called *The Maid of the Mist* was placed, facing him, at the corner of his desk. They were all wearing blue rain slickers.

Fogarty was an expert at figuring out fire patterns and knowing precisely where the point of origin was. The fire in Mrs. LeBrun's house was not difficult to determine. Detective Fogarty dismissed this case as an unfortunate routine accident and spoke to Mrs. LeBrun in a low matter of fact tone.

"Your husband took to smoking a lot of cigars. We found at least a hundred stubs strewn throughout your house," he said. "My guess, and I'd say it's dead-on accurate, is that your husband fell asleep while watching television letting a lit cigar fall from his hand and roll under his bed. It smoldered on the carpet for a long time and then very quickly flames built and caught underneath his mattress which went up in flames in no time. Your husband was too large to move quickly enough to get away."

Mrs. LeBrun sat apprehensively before Detective Fogarty breathing in the stale air of his tiny office. She shuddered at the thought of her husband alone in his room burning. She imagined Mr. LeBrun unable to roll from the bed and for some odd reason she could not get it out of her mind that his blood must have reached a boiling point until he exploded and his innards hissed and squealed and burned until he was no more.

Fogarty eased back in his chair and crossed his arms signaling there was no more to say about the matter. It was a simple case. A simple case of stupidity and misfortune, he thought to himself.

"Why didn't the firemen get my husband out of the house?" Mrs. LeBrun asked.

"When the trucks arrived at the scene, the inside of the house was totally engulfed in fire. Your husband was a very large man," he said. "The second floor gave way and your husband and everything else collapsed into the first floor. The fire was so hot and contained inside the brick walls that everything just incinerated into ash. Your husband included. There was really no way to retrieve him, Mrs. LeBrun."

Mrs. LeBrun thanked Detective Fogarty and hastily left his office. Outside on the street the air was warm and the day was bright. The sky was a crisp radiant topaz blue. Mrs. LeBrun stood on the corner, opened her purse, reached for her phone, and called her good friend Diane. Diane promised to contact Mary Alice and the three of them would rent a villa in Italy. They could spend the days walking on the sand and swimming in the sea.

"It would be warm and refreshing," Diane said.

KiLL Me

There are many ways for me to walk to work, but I prefer to stroll down Elmwood Avenue. It takes approximately fifteen minutes to get from my apartment to my job. I work behind the counter at the Mobil Mart selling crap to people who pump their gas and come into the store to buy lottery tickets or cigarettes or beer or a quick bite of something shitty like Hostess Twinkies or a bag of chips. I sell a whole bunch of lottery tickets and, in the three years since I've worked here, I can't remember anyone winning a dime. The place is constantly busy. There're always people in the joint. The Mobil Mart sits on a busy intersection right across the street from the Buffalo Psychiatric Center, so we get a lot of those nut-jobs strolling in, too.

Luckily, we've never been robbed. Probably because we have cameras all over the place. As soon as someone steps foot on the property they're being filmed, so they know better than pulling something stupid and getting caught. Some of the crack-bastards that hang around the neighborhood will steal stuff like candy bars off of the shelves, but I don't pay them any attention and I'm sure not going risk my ass going after them.

As I said, there are many ways to walk to work, but I usually take Elmwood. I would rather drive, but I got nailed a while back for my third DWI, and the judge took my license away for a long time. I did three months in the County jail. They locked me up for ploughing into a couple of parked cars while I was drunk. I didn't have any money for bail or anything, so I just took the rap and hung in jail till they let me out. No big deal. Jail isn't bad, at least the one downtown isn't.

I was glad that when I got out Darryl gave me my job back. He's the guy who runs the Mobil Mart. Darryl doesn't give a damn about working here anyhow; he just shows up for a little bit in the afternoon to check things out, make sure everything's running smoothly. The store is open all day and all night. I work Monday through Friday from seven in the morning until three in the afternoon. It's a good shift. When I'm not working, I'm writing for a couple of local papers here in town, mostly political stuff or about scandals going on here in the neighborhood. Sometimes they throw me a few bucks and I get to review a cheap restaurant or a bar. They give the good restaurants to a reviewer they have on staff.

He writes like a pompous jerk-off. It doesn't pay hardly anything, but I like to do it. Write that is.

I could take the side streets. I could walk up Ashland or Norwood and look at those nice, big Victorian houses. The streets are loaded with giant oak and elm trees and in the summer they really throw a lot of shade. In the fall the colors are beautiful: gold, red, burnt orange, and in the winter they're leafless dull brown and twisted like the arms of naked, brittle old ladies. Sometimes I do take those streets, but like I said, I would rather walk down Elmwood to get to work.

*****

When you walk down the same street at the same time every day you see the same people doing the same thing. Everyone's in a routine. I leave my apartment at six-thirty sharp. The people I see are either jogging or heading to work or school or somewhere like that. A lot of times I run into this wild-eyed, crazy old black guy sleeping under a filthy tattered blanket, curled up like a baby, in the doorway of the cheese shop. Later in the day he'll be strutting up and down Elmwood, hi-fiving anyone who'll let him, hollering and bugging passersby for money. Another I run across is this short, tiny, grimy drunk who exists perpetually in a booze haze. He can be spotted anywhere: digging through garbage cans, weaving in place on some corner, or sitting in some doorway sloppily rolling a smoke. When I walk by he raises his arm toward me and tries to spit something out, but he's too slow to get any words flowing and I'm not about to wait around for his babbling nonsense. There are a couple more early morning loonies that get out of the Psychiatric Center bright and early and hit the street. They're usually not a problem. Like I said, most are people walking or waiting for a bus to take them to work or school.

I always head north along the dark street on the east side of Elmwood. None of the businesses are open at that time except for a couple of coffee shops and the 7-Eleven and, of course, The Mobil Mart.

*****

They say Buffalo's a friendly town. One thing is for certain, most people have the decency to muster up a *hello* when you pass them on the street. Every morning I get a nod from a big black woman who waits at the bus stop with a scrawny white chick and a short round Puerto Rican guy who wears a red beret. They always give me a nod or a wave. Joggers usually raise their hand when passing. Everyone shares that quick glance of recognition. That is, everyone except for this one girl who passes by me every day and does not acknowledge me in the slightest.

I see her coming every morning right about the time I pass a place called Blue Monk, one of those trendy and expensive craft beer joints. I hear they have good food and about a hundred beers to choose from. The place is always packed in the evenings with a lotta guys in tight flannel shirts with thick beards and colorful tattoos covering their arms, and the joint is loaded with chicks with hair dyed jet-black or auburn-red and wearing skinny jeans and sporting just as many tattoos.

Every single morning she avoids looking at me by keeping her head tilted toward the sidewalk and moving straight on by. It's as if she's determined *not* to see me, to purposely ignore me. She never really bothered me much until, for some reason over time, she really started pissing me off. I mean, I walk by her every day and she can't even bother to look up and acknowledge me? I clench my fists and mutter something god-awful when she hurries by. She passes me as if I don't exist, like I'm a flea or a gnat or maybe a potato bug. I try to make eye contact with her. No way, she won't have it. She glides by like I'm nothing, a worthless piece of shit. I thought of walking up the other side of Elmwood so I wouldn't have to deal with her blatant abuse and then I thought, "The hell with that…

why should I?"

By the time I get to work, I forget about her. I have too much to do. Dan, the guy who works the eleven-to-seven shift, immediately throws me the inventory sheet letting me know what needs to be stocked. It's usually not much. In the mornings the trucks pull in and make their deliveries. The beer truck makes the most deliveries, then the food guys and everyone else who sells their stuff in here. Mornings between seven and nine are pretty busy, so I forget about her for the most part.

For a while I didn't see her. Her schedule must have changed. It must have been a good month later, while I was walking to work, I saw her approaching in the distance. It was right as I was passing Blue Monk. She did the same thing—put her head down, picked up her pace, and tore past me without even a glance in my direction. Who does she think she is?!

One afternoon she came into the Mobil Mart. I stood behind the counter watching her, my heart pounding. Her skin was delicate and pale. She went about her business without acknowledging anyone in the store. She gave no friendly nods of greeting, nothing. She grabbed a newspaper from the stack in the bin. She went into the cooler and grabbed one of those bottles of unsweetened green iced teas, too. As I was ringing her up, she glanced toward me. I looked into her soft green eyes. She didn't recognize me, didn't have a damn clue that I passed her every morning. I placed her seventy-five cents change into her upturned palm and thanked her. She turned around and walked out, not saying a thing. My heart exploded! Pompous arrogant bitch!

I couldn't stop thinking of her. Her existence consumed me. I knew there was no reason to obsess about one uptight broad who ignored me day after day, but I could not get her out of my head. Who was she? What was she all about? I needed to know.

The next time I ran into her, she walked by with her head down avoiding my glance. This time I stopped, turned in her direction, and followed her. She moved onward straight and steady. She was a fast walker. She entered the Starbucks on Elmwood. I discovered that she worked there. I continued watching her for days and learned that her shift ended at four o'clock, one hour past mine.

A few days later, I got the nerve to go into the Starbucks. It was around three-fifteen and I ordered a tall black coffee. I don't drink any of those fancy frappe coffees. A skinny girl with cropped black hair and cherry-red lipstick worked the counter. My interest made the fancy drinks that the counter girl called out to her. She didn't make mine; the cashier could handle a black coffee. I sat at a table near the counter reading a newspaper and watching her. She moved quietly with determined precision. Her lips were tightly planted while she concentrated. Her countenance remained dull and focused.

She continued to pass me on the street, continued to ignore me, continued to walk past me quickly, and determined not to notice me. But, I knew where she worked and now I was going to find out where she lived, that was for sure.

*****

There are a lot of residential streets that branch of Elmwood Avenue. Most of the houses are large two story flats with big front porches. She lived two doors down from a corner dry cleaner in an upper flat. It was a pretty good sized place. Her front porch was covered with a forest green awning and she had wicker furniture and a whole bunch of plants and herbs and vegetables growing in wooden buckets. She must relax there on summer evenings while the sun is going down, I thought.

There was comfort in knowing a little bit more about her, now. I knew where she worked and I knew where she lived. Not bad, a good start, but I needed to know more. What got this girl lit up? What got her out of her miserable funk? Who did she hang with? Where did she go? Was she intelligent? I thought maybe she was, maybe she was always thinking profound intellectual thoughts; maybe she was captured deep in some crazy thought process that got a hold of her and wouldn't let go. Maybe she was an artist. Or, was she just a bitch? Either way, I aimed to learn more about her.

I was right. In the evenings she sat on her porch quietly absorbed in some book. She seldom looked up from whatever she was reading. There was that defiant determination to ignore me again. I would *happen* to walk down her street; *happen* to glance cautiously up toward her gathering as much information as I could, careful not to be noticed. I figured if I passed at the same time every day she would imagine my walking-by as simply routine, as if I had a purpose, as if I needed to be somewhere and this was my way of getting there, always.

One early evening I passed by while she was deeply engaged in some book. I glanced upward trying desperately to steal a look, careful not to appear obvious. Suddenly, she set her book down and focused directly on me. She looked at me; she looked through me! I was stuck! She saw me! I mustered a weak wave acknowledging our mutual connection and she paused for the slightest moment sizing me up and then she lifted that book and put her nose right back in it. That bitch!

It was clear now. She was toying with me. She was playing me like a goddamned fiddle. She knew who I was. My stomach tightened. She noticed me every morning when I passed by her. How could she not? I walked by her daily; we were only inches apart. She chose to ignore me, figured she was better than me. The goddamn book reading intellect! Who the hell did she think I was, just some schmuck working at a lousy Mobil Mart? That's what she thought and I knew it! I walked down her street and I passed by her house and every time I looked up, her nose was crammed in that book. She saw me coming and she ignored me. She purposely ignored me just to show me she was better than me, that I was a turd and that's a goddamned fact!

*****

There are many bars and restaurants on Elmwood Avenue, and in the evenings most tables and barstools are filled. I don't go out too much during the week, but every once in a while, on a Friday night, I'll hit one of the places for a bite and a few beers. I don't waste my money on the fancy joints. There are a lot of solid dives in the neighborhood with good food and cheap drinks that suit me just fine.

I hadn't seen her in a while. I had to get away. I was sick of her ignoring me. Truth is, she was chewing me up inside, so instead of taking Elmwood, I changed my routine and walked to work by going down Ashland Avenue past the big houses under the sprawling elm trees. I stopped walking past her place in the evenings too.

It was the beginning of October and the leaves were turning bright red, orange, and yellow. The early evening air was cooler, so I figured she wouldn't be hanging on her porch anyway. I felt better. And so, I had all but forgotten about her until, while sitting on a corner barstool, at the noisy and crowded Place Bar & Restaurant, enjoying a roast beef dinner with mashed potatoes and gravy, and drinking a pint of Guinness, she and another girl sashayed right into the joint, pulling up a couple of empty stools, and plunking themselves right next to me. She turned toward me and mustered a polite smile, then went back to her friend. They took off their jackets, settled in, and contemplated what to order. My head felt light and my ears got fiery hot. The two of them leaned into one another in deep conversation. She kept her back to me.

"Hey Julie, it's nice to see you," Franny said, wiping his fat meaty hands on a bar towel lying flat against his shoulder before extending his pudgy fingers and taking hers. Franny took their order and poured two tall beers and placed them on coasters on the bar before them.

"Nice crowd," she said.

Franny surveyed the dining room. Every table was full and most of the bar was full too.

"Dinner crowd," he said. "The bar will pick up later on."

"This is Paula," she said.

Paula extended her hand toward Franny and gave him a courteous smile.

"Hi," Paula said.

"Let me know what you gals need," Franny said. "Menus?"

"That would be great, Franny," she said.

So, her name was Julie. I guess it's a name as good as any other. She looked a little looser tonight, not so uptight, a little made up. A slight touch of lipstick gave her lips a rosy hue and her eyes held a thin trace of eyeliner around them. She primped herself in a subtle manner, didn't overdo it. Had on a pair of blue jeans and a black sweater tight enough to show her shape nicely, small and round up top.

The Place carried a noisy and annoying hum in the air; a mix of conversation, laughter and the general loudness of a bunch of people eating in a crammed room. The two of them huddled into one another, deep in conversation, as if they were the only two in the room, as if they were the only two people on the whole planet, for that matter.

It was too loud to make out what they were saying. It must have been good, though; they didn't come up for air. I became agitated. Was she talking about me? Was she telling her friend her cruel joke of ignoring me? At one point they stopped talking and looked in my direction, and then they looked over the menus. They decided and Franny took their orders. He returned a little later with a burger for the friend and a fish-fry for her. He brought them another couple of those tall beers too.

They took their time eating and kept close to one another, giggling, smirking, and sharing their cruel secrets. They ordered another beer. I finished my dinner and ordered another Guinness. I wasn't going to miss keeping my eye on her for anything.

They took their time eating and when they finished, Franny took their plates and wiped the bar before them. I sipped my Guinness and kept my eye on her. I ordered two shots of Paddy Irish whiskey and Franny and I knocked them back. Franny grimaced and thanked me by pouring another pint and placing it before me. I moved a fiver in his direction. He picked it up and placed it in the register.

I needed to talk to her, but I wasn't going to open my mouth. What would I say? I never was one to start a conversation with a chick at a bar. I don't have the same confidence as a lot of guys. I guess you'd say I'm not a smooth talker. Besides, these two were so wrapped up in themselves, it was apparent they weren't interested in shooting the shit with anyone else. That is until Paula suddenly stood up and headed toward the bathroom and this Julie turned toward me, throwing a sly smile in my direction. Her eyes locked onto mine and I noticed her cheeks were slightly flushed giving them a light ruddy glow.

"It's really loud in here, she said. "I can barely hear myself think."

"You know The Place; it's always busy this time of year."

"Are you waiting for someone?" she asked.

What the hell was she doing? What was her trick, to play me a fool? I figured I'd play it cool; see where she was going to take this. Besides, I didn't have much of a plan anyway.

"No, I'm just having a bite and a couple of beers."

"And a shot…I watched you and Franny have a shot. I like shots once in a while. Do you want to do one?

Do you want to do one with me?" she asked, looking unwavering into my eyes.

"I could handle another Paddy," I said.

"I've never heard of Paddy."

"It's Irish Whiskey."

"Jameson I've had, but never Paddy," she said.

"It's a lot smoother than Jameson. It's more popular in Ireland. Jameson's more popular world-wide, but the Irish like the Paddy better," I said.

"Let's have one," she said, smiling and looking right into me, looking right through me, mocking me, toying with me, playing me for a fool. "I'll get one for my friend. I bet she would like one too."

"I'm Julie," she said extending her hand in my direction. I took her hand into mine. It was firm and strong and she held a tight grip. My old man used to tell me, 'shake hands firmly like a man, son; you can tell a wimp by the way a man shakes his hand.' Hers was firm and full of confidence.

"Tom," I said returning her hand.

"Tom, who?"

"Sweeny," I said. "Tom Sweeny."

"Nice Polish name," she said, and giggled.

Paula returned and noticed the shot in front of her.

"It's Paddy," Julie said. "It's more popular than

Jameson in Ireland."

We drank the shots. Julie tilted her head back taking the shot without the slightest hint of a sour face. She was savoring the flavor, really tasting the whiskey.

"I like that," she said, looking at me. "It's very smooth like you said."

Paula agreed and the two of them sat turned in my direction and told me a few things about themselves like they've been friends for years, went to the same grammar school, School #45 on the West Side of Buffalo, and they both went to college right here at Buffalo State. Paula studied social work and Julie studied English.

"How about you?" Julie asked. "What do you do Tom Sweeny?"

"Not much," I said. "I work at the Mobil Mart down on Elmwood across from the Psychiatric Center and I write for the Reserve and sometimes the News, mostly political stuff, restaurant reviews, nothing much."

"So you're an intellectual and a thinker! I bet you're a deep thinker; I bet you think way too much," Julie said, with a warm smile and looking damn good in that tight sweater.

"You might say," I said, ordering us three more shots of Paddy and a back-up on our beers.

"I don't know what I'll do with an English degree,

maybe teach, but I don't want to teach. I got a degree in English because I love literature. I love to read. I have to figure it out. At least I got my degree and that's good for something, I hope." she said.

Paula turned to her right and picked up a conversation with a couple of college looking guys. They both had on flannel shirts and were drinking porters in pint glasses. It seemed she knew them from another time.

"I wish I could write," she continued. "I did some writing in school. I took a creative writing class and wrote a story about a lonely old man living with a smelly six-toed dog. In the story he comes home from his shitty job, drinks a bottle of cheap whiskey, stabs his dog with a kitchen knife, turns the gas on in his oven, puts his head in it, and kills himself. My professor said he liked the description of the dog, but the story itself was mundane and predictable. How about you? What do you write?"

"I don't tell stories. I just write about stuff that's going on like crime in the neighborhood or politicians who get nothing done, or those bicyclists who think they own the road. I'd like to knock a few of them in their place." I said.

"You're raw; now I recognize your name. I've read your articles. It's really edgy stuff and your restaurant reviews are hilarious. You say some pretty nasty things if the food is lousy."

"I've gotten in trouble for that," I said. "I figure if someone has a restaurant, then they should have good food. It's what they're supposed to be good at. They've been keeping me away from the restaurants lately."

"So, the Mobil Mart is just a place to work until you're a Pulitzer Prize winning journalist, right?"

"You might say," I said.

She inched herself closer, bending her head nearer to mine. I breathed in a faint hint of powdery perfume; she smelled clean and fresh. Her knee pushed gently against my leg and her eyes locked firmly onto mine. Paula continued her conversation with the two college boys who bought us all a shot. Julie and I did a Paddy and the other three knocked back a Jägermeister. I ordered another beer for myself and Julie and I watched her face slowly melt before me like tallowed wax. Her lips were shiny, her eyes glossy, and her cheeks held a flaming radiance.

She was playing me for a fool and that was a fact. I wasn't going to stand for it and I figured I'd better get out of there fast. Besides, the continuous clamoring from the crowd was irritating the hell out of me. I couldn't focus on what she was saying. I only heard the amplified swell of other voices loud and laughing like a cacophony of endless madness. I needed air and I needed to get out.

I waved Franny over giving him the signal that I wanted the check.

"Are you leaving?" Julie asked.

"I have to. It's too loud in here; I can't concentrate," I said.

I figured if I left now, everything would be okay. I could get along without her. I needed to know nothing more. She was a bore and I knew enough, besides the next time I passed her on the street she would acknowledge me. She may even consider me an acquaintance. She may even stop to chat, who knows? I couldn't deal with that. I began thinking of other ways to walk to the Mobil Mart.

"My place isn't far from here," she said. "I have some beer at home. You're right; this place is too loud. I can barely hear myself think."

How far was she going to go? I wondered.

*****

She kept the overhead light off and clicked on a couple of antique table lamps. The bulbs were low wattage and the room mellowed in a soft orange glow. Her apartment was spacious with dark hardwood floors, oak archways, and bookcases with cut-glass doors built into the walls of the living room. She had a lot of books stuffed into those shelves. I noticed a couple of long-haired black and white cats sliding quietly into the living room.

"Beer or wine?" she asked.

"I haven't thought about it. What are you having?"

"I would like a glass of red wine, but you can have whatever you'd like."

"Wine sounds fine," I said.

I sat on her big sofa while she went into the kitchen. I had a tight, hollow pit in my gut, and I felt slightly dizzy and uneasy. What was she after? Why did she leave her friend? Something was not right. She returned with a bottle of wine and two short juice glasses.

"My dad calls these goomba glasses. It's what Italians use to drink every-day wine," she said, pouring the wine into the glasses.

She raised her glass and we touched them lightly and she melted comfortably into the sofa keeping her eyes on me. Unexpectedly, I watched her eyes grow heavy. Her hand tilted slightly almost pouring some of the wine onto her legs. I took the wine glass from her and watched her sleep, silently, delicately. I stayed with her and drank the wine until I had finished the bottle, and then I sat in the stillness of her quiet apartment, in the warm glow of the orange lighting, listening to the repetitions of her breath softly and slowly moving from her.

I figured I would slip out the door and let her sleep. I rose gently from the sofa and she opened her eyes and grasped my arm.

"Take me in the other room," she said.

She had a large bed with a big puffy white quilt. She slid her clothes off and stood naked and silent before me. Then she slipped under the covers and into the bed.

"Take off your clothes and come in."

She moved to the center of the bed and pulled me to her. Very slowly she reached down, while opening her legs, and pulled me into her. She moved into me gently, steadily and deliberately.

"I've watched you walking in the morning," she said thrusting her hips forward allowing longer strokes. "I've seen you at your work and I've watched you walk by my house and look up at me many times."

She moved faster clamping down on me. Her breath getting shorter, holding onto my shoulders, I could feel her tightening.

"Why did you ignore me?" I asked.

"Because," she said. "Because, I knew you were going to kill me."

The WaterFall

T he road was not paved. They had been driving close to an hour. Rose dangled her arm delicately out of the window. She leaned back and breathed in the wet-slate scented air.

"Now, this is where I love to be," Rose said. "Listen, what do you hear?"

"Nothing," Peter said.

"I know, I love it," she said, settling comfortably in the passenger seat.

It had rained the night before and the sun's rays had not completely penetrated and dried the thick woods. Trees stood swollen and wet and the winding muddy road lay scattered with large ruts filled with brown water. The road was taking them closer to the river. Peter could hear the strong hum of water rushing in the distance, and he knew it was running too fast and muddy for trout.

"I hope we haven't forgotten anything," Rose said. "Let's see…wine, food, our sleeping bags, matches, the tarp, the tent, fishing gear…"

"I have the camera; I think we're all set," Peter said.

"Good," Rose said. "We have everything and more."

They had come from their home in the village of Springville nestled in the Boston Hills of Western New York. But now they were miles further and had turned off the paved road and onto a puddled and muddy road leading them to their favorite campsite. It was getting hot. The sun had risen higher. It was big and bright. The sky held long delicate wisps of cotton white clouds.

They were getting closer to their campsite and listened to the deep sound of the waterfall in the distance. Once they reached the camp they would hike to the falls and stand on the large bank looking over the steady flow of water pounding over smooth gray boulders. They would feel the cool spray from the strength of the water and they always had to shout over the thunderous roar to hear one another.

The river twisted and wandered for miles; neither knew how long it actually was. The river was loaded with brown trout and rainbow trout and they could usually fish out ones of good size. They arrived to where the road ended. Peter parked the car under the shade of a wide-hanging willow tree.

"Okay," Peter said. "We'll walk from here."

By this time the sun burned high in the sky and the water had dried from the trees. They listened to the hollow buzzing of bees and large horse-flies. They took their gear from the car and laid it on the ground. Peter had packed well. There was not much to carry.

The walk to the camp was only about a mile. Peter had his camera strapped around his neck. There was nothing difficult about the hike, except that they had to cross the creek. If the creek was not too high, and there were plenty of rocks, they could cross easily without getting wet. But, it had rained heavily the night before and by the fast moving sound of the river, the creek would also be high. It did not matter. They could take off their shoes and the water would not go much past their knees.

"Are you ready?" Peter asked.

"Yes, let's go," Rose replied.

Rose walked ahead. She was a lovely sight and looked even more stunning to Peter in the woods, alone. Peter snapped a series of photos of Rose along the way using the sun as his natural light. The light bathed her in a warm, clear glow. She posed and smiled, her eyes brilliantly lit. When they reached the creek it was deep, muddy and fast moving. They crossed the creek and the water came up to their waists, higher than ever before. The water moved furiously and almost knocked them down. They reached the opposite side and sat on the bank to dry and rest for a while. They were in no hurry. Peter snapped more photos. Rose posed. There was plenty of time.

"I could sit here forever, but I know that isn't right because our camp is even more beautiful and high-up and looking over the waterfall," Rose said. "I love to look at the waterfall, and I love to bathe in it, and I love me when I'm there because I'm myself and I can be myself when I'm with you."

"You sure talk funny, Rose," Peter said.

"I do not. I'm happy to be here. I'm so happy we have this weekend. There's nobody here except us. We can do whatever we want. Anything we want to do, we can."

"What do you have in mind, Rose?"

"Come on, let's go to the camp," Rose said, getting up and taking his hand.

They hiked up a large wooded hill and came to an open meadow. The bright sun warmed the back of their necks. Bees hovered busily over raspberry bushes scattered throughout the bright-golden meadow. The berries were perfectly ripe and Rose and Peter picked and ate the sweet fruit as they moved forward. They passed through the meadow and reached another wooded area. It was cooler in the deeper woods and the sun rays made surreal, luminous lines through the trees. The woods smelled rich and wet. The soil was soft with grassy spots. Purple and yellow wild flowers covered the ground and spread in every direction. There were many tall trees and many hollowed fallen ones. The sound of the waterfall grew deeper and louder. They only had to walk down a steep wooded hill to their camp.

They made it down quickly and they were excited. They had arrived at the camp that looked over the waterfall. The ground was damp, but only slightly. There was plenty of fallen firewood all around and the loose pieces scattered on top were dry enough to start a fire. No one had camped in these woods in a long while. It was very clean. The only evidence of past campers was a series of rocks forming a circle to make a campfire. Later, Peter and Rose would have a strong fire.

They unloaded the gear and Peter began putting up the tent. He rolled it out and pounded the stakes easily into the soft ground. Rose helped scatter some of the gear, but became more interested in wandering toward the waterfall. She stood over the waterfall and watched the silvery curve thrashing hard and wild into the river below. The water rushed down the river, churning white as it hurled its journeys length over the boulders and through the open air. The spray from the water covered her in a cool glistening sheen. When the water reached the bottom, it whirl-pooled, and then gently, like a zephyr, continued down the river very slowly.

On the other side of the waterfall a steep slate-gray cliff rose sharply above. At the top of the cliff, thick woods with tall trees under soft-blue skies were spread before her.

Peter finished setting up the tent and arranged the gear in its proper place. He started a small fire and made coffee. He brought the steaming dark coffee in tin cups handing one to Rose. The coffee tasted good. They stood silently overlooking the endlessly pounding waterfall. It was a good day for them.

Time passes. An old man stands alone in slippers and a bathrobe, quietly looking at a picture of his wife, long dead, framed on a table in their living room. It is one photo among many. He looks at it closely. She is standing gracefully in front of a brilliant waterfall. Her eyes are bright. She is posing for the camera and making a funny face at him.

"It was so many, many years ago," he reminisced, thinking of his beautiful Rose and the vivid timelessness of the waterfall.

A Restaurant Needs Publicity

After the last table of guests cleared, Donald Parker still had about an hour left to take inventory, count the money, and wait for Roberto, his dishwasher, to finish mopping the floor so he could lock the doors before heading out. When that was taken care of, he put on his jacket and walked around the corner under a dark sky and misty rain to meet his new waitress Anita. Earlier in the evening Anita mentioned to Parker that she was planning to head over to Mother's Restaurant after her shift and she *insisted* that he meet her there. Parker was fond of her and looked forward to their meeting.

A chilly breeze pushed through the dark city. The rich earthy smell of autumn hung heavily in the wet evening air and miniature cyclones of leaves scattered aimlessly across the shiny wet street. Parker entered the restaurant and was disappointed to see an old acquaintance named Jeff throwing back a shot of tequila with Anita.

Parker knew Jeff from another time and knew what a sly fucker he was. He didn't expect to see him there, not with her. His thoughts immediately turned to getting rid of this guy so he could have time alone with Anita.

It wasn't until quite some time later that Parker knew the circumstances of their meeting: Anita had been working at the restaurant for a little over a week. She was new to Buffalo, came up from Jamestown armed with a BA in Art and a plan to paint her way to fame and fortune. She met Jeff a couple of weeks earlier while sitting at a sidewalk table in front of Spot Coffee. It was an unusually balmy autumn day. Anita took in the soft afternoon sun, drawing intently on a sketch pad, when Jeff strolled down the sidewalk and noticed her alone and concentrating on her drawings. He nosed in, commented on her *incredible* talent, boldly sat down at her table, and tried to impress her with his limited knowledge of art he learned in an art appreciation class in high school. She figured he was pleasant enough, not much of a threat, and allowed him to sit with her while they sipped on cups of French roast coffee.

Parker knew differently, knew what a piece of shit he was, knew that they had problems in the past, and knew that he wanted Jeff out of the picture.

Mother's was crowded. It was always crowded and it got in full swing later in the evening, after midnight, when restaurant workers - cooks, waiters, bartenders, arrived from their shifts for a late-night dinner. Mother's served a full menu until at least three in the morning and their food was some of the best in town. Parker moved through the crowd, and slid up to the bar to join them.

"Well, look who's here…Donald Parker restaurant extraordinaire. It's been awhile," Jeff said, extending his hand and offering a dry smile.

Parker took his hand and gave it an overly firm shake.

"It has been awhile," Parker said.

"How 'bout a drink, pal? What can I get you?" Jeff said.

"I'll take a Molson and a shot of Jameson," Parker said. "You two look like you're ahead of me."

"A little bit," Jeff agreed.

Anita sat on a barstool, her hair hanging dark and loosely over her shoulders. Thick eyebrows gave her deep brown eyes a shadowy hue. She held onto a glass of white wine and Jeff was drinking something mixed with soda.

Parker knocked back the Jameson and surveyed the room. Along with the restaurant workers, good-look-ing women draped on barstools in chic dresses and high heels sat surrounded by lustful men in tailored suits, pressed slacks, and shiny shoes. Parker held his gaze firmly on Jeff standing before him, handsome, crisp, and dark-haired.

"So, when did you get out of the crowbar hotel?" Parker asked.

"Come on Don, I don't want to talk about that," Jeff said with an uneasy smile.

"What's the crowbar hotel?" Anita asked.

"Jeff got a little time for some telemarketing fraud," Parker said. "Weren't you scamming little old ladies or something like that? Didn't I read something in the paper about you inflating prices on things like key chains and vitamins and water purifiers and telling suckers they would be entered into a contest where they'd win diamond bracelets and Cadillac's if they bought your junk? Nobody ever won anything; they just got fooled into buying a lot of cheap shit at inflated prices."

"That wasn't my company; I just worked there. I didn't know anything about fraud."

"You ended up going to jail for it, so I guess you must have known something," Parker said.

"That was a couple of years ago," Jeff said, shifting uneasily. "I'm not doing that anymore."

"Well, good for you; I'm just kidding with you,"

Parker said, thinking to himself how much he'd like to slug this guy in the face. At another time, in the past, he probably would have, but he was working hard to control those urges. None of that behavior ever solved anything, really. Those days had gotten him into more trouble than he cared to remember.

In the height of the scamming, Jeff was living pretty well off. He had an attractive wife, a big house in Spaulding Lake, his and her BMWs, and a couple of vintage Indian motorcycles. He lived in a wardrobe of custom made Italian suits from Napoli's Men's Shop. After three years in jail and paying a restitution of close to 1.2 million dollars, Jeff was broke and starting over. Parker heard his wife had split to Miami while he was in jail. He also knew that Jeff was the type of bastard that would always land on his feet, no matter what. He had that type of personality; he knew people. He would dismiss his past crimes as an error in judgement, a stupid mistake, a learning opportunity, "I guess I have to learn the hard way," he'd say.

Parker knew this same group that scammed old ladies had regrouped and was buying cheap properties on the East Side and the Lower West Side of Buffalo, flipping the properties, buying more, buying bigger, buying commercial and making a shit-load of money, and sly fucker

Jeff was right back in the center of the action.

"How about we all have a shot?" Jeff said. "Something easy?"

"I don't think so, that tequila feels like it's still stuck in my throat. I don't do well with shots," Anita said.

"How about you, Don?" Jeff asked.

"Sure, something easy. I'll have another Jameson," Parker said.

"Well, I don't know how easy that is, but I'll match you," Jeff said, and ordered two shots of Jameson and two Molson Canadians to chase them down.

Anita sipped her wine slowly.

Donald Parker shifted uneasily at the bar. His plans of meeting Anita alone, getting a table, a bite to eat, a bottle of wine, were spoiled by Jeff's arrival. He liked Anita and wanted to know her better. But, now he was drinking shots at the bar. His mood was stifled by this jerk-off and he wanted nothing more than to hurt him.

Jeff spoke about his latest ventures, buying properties, fixing them up, flipping them for a profit. He explained his plans to extend the business to Florida and sell properties to the snow birds. The evening wore on and as Jeff spoke, Parker listened with a disdained ear, feeling a tumultuous tension building at his core. His left eye involuntarily twitching the longer Jeff dragged out his stories.

It seemed Jeff was acquainted with just about everyone walking in or out of the restaurant. Many gave him a nod of recognition, a hand shake, or a pat on the back. When a woman walked past, Jeff's gaze would undress her from the ankles up. His thoughts wide open for all to see, each girl lying naked on a bed captured in Jeff's desires.

A few feet from where they were standing a group of slick-dressed men with shiny black hair and crooked smiles waved Jeff over giving Parker an opportunity to nestle closer to Anita at the bar. He was relieved he had disappeared and given him time alone with Anita, at least for a moment, but he could think of nothing witty or intimate to share with her. The mood was gone. He absently engaged in dismally forced small talk about the restaurant, what a decent night it was, and how he particularly enjoyed making the lobster with vanilla bean butter as a special. He felt foolishly out of place standing amongst these polished people wearing a dingy corduroy shirt, brown loafers and a worn pair of Levi's.

Parker ordered another Jameson and a Molson. "I think I'm a little underdressed for this place," Parker said.

"Me too," Anita said. "But, I don't mind. I feel re-laxed just being out and knowing I have a couple of days off."

"I'm glad you're working at the restaurant."

"Thanks," Anita said. "I like it and your food is really fantastic."

"I wish everyone thought the same thing," Parker said. "I mean, everyone gets reviews, articles written about them. I know a lot of chefs that are hacks and they get mentioned in the paper as something great."

"Call the Buffalo News and ask for a review," Anita said. "That's the way it works. If you wait, it may never come."

"You have a point."

"In art, you have to hustle to get attention. You have to send out press releases, stay constant on social media. It's a pain, really."

Donald Parker saw a calm determination in Anita's eyes. He wanted to take her to his place and lie down with her pressing comfortably into him. He knew that wasn't going to happen, not now. That mood was lost and he felt the cunning eyes of Jeff watching them in his peripheral. Jeff had his own ideas of what he would like to do to Anita. Parker was repulsed at the thought of Jeff closing in on Anita. Jeff would peg her once, and then toss her out into the night without a thought.

"We can go back to the restaurant and open a

bottle of wine," Parker whispered to Anita. "I'm a little hungry and I could cook something up for us pretty fast."

"That would be nice," Anita said.

Parker tipped back the Molson, letting the rest of it quickly slide down his throat. The instant he placed the bottle on the bar, Jeff was standing before them.

"Sorry I left," he said. "I had to talk to those guys, they're friends of mine. So, what's going on? Where are you heading?"

Parker latched onto him with a furrowed brow and flat, glazed eyes. "This place is too crowded; we're going back to the restaurant where it's quieter."

Jeff felt Parker's intense dislike for him. He observed Parker's wide head, thick lips, and Neanderthal figure. Parker had fists the size of flour sacks and Jeff knew if Parker had his way, he'd pummel him with every bit of energy he could muster. Jeff had seen Parker use them before, he knew he had an anger buried deep within, and he'd seen the mighty wrath of Parker, temper lost, pounding some poor sucker with relentless fury. Parker was famous for that and Jeff was famous for taking chances, toying with people. He wanted Anita only for the night, but more than that, he wanted to take her from Donald Parker before Parker even had a chance. That would be a fun game...the real score, he figured.

"I agree," Jeff said. "It is too crowded in here; let's go."

*****

Donald Parker pulled the wad of keys from his jacket pocket, fumbled to find the right one, and unsteadily slid it into the rear door of his restaurant. Parker entered through the kitchen with his new waitress Anita and smart-ass Jeff. He was slightly buzzed from the Jameson and the beers. They moved into the dining room. Parker turned on some lights, dimming them and softening the room. He lit a candle and pulled a bottle of wine from the rack. The three of them settled at the table closest to the kitchen.

"This should work," he said pouring a little wine into each of the three glasses.

Jeff swirled his glass letting the wine coat the inside. He placed his nose deep inside the wide bowl and breathed in. Then, he tilted his head back and took a slow pull letting it rest in his mouth before swallowing.

"Nice," he said. "Very nice."

"It's an Amarone," Parker said. "It has a bit of a fig preserve flavor."

"Yes, very nice," Jeff said and placed his eyes on Anita before beginning to speak. "You know, Parker and

I go way back. We worked in restaurants together maybe twenty years ago. Wouldn't you say?"

"It's been that long," Parker agreed.

"You were one crazy bastard," Jeff said. "Remember the time you leveled that guy down at The Rendezvous Bar on Niagara Street? We were sitting at that table and he reached over to get a cigarette from your pocket and you smashed him right in the face with your fist. Man, blood splattered everywhere."

"That was a long time ago, Jeff. Besides, I told him he couldn't have one and he reached over the table anyway and stuffed his hand in my pocket. He was a friend of yours if I remember."

"I remember you told me you were banging this broad and when she came she would laugh hysterically and scratch your back until you bled. You said you had to hide your back from your girlfriend."

Parker grew increasingly irritated. He knew the score. Jeff's tactics were too god-dammed obvious- make Anita believe Parker was a raging lunatic, bust him down and shred him up in his own restaurant. Drink his wine, eat his food, take his girl, and have a good laugh about it later. That would be a great story to tell those faceless friends of his.

Jeff inched closer to Anita. She backed slightly

away from his advances sipping her wine and searching for something to say.

"I guess it's always nice when old friends get together," Anita said.

"I agree," Jeff said, raising his glass and locking eyes on Parker. "It's always nice when old friends get together. Isn't it, Donald?"

"I wouldn't say old *friends;* we've known each other a long time, but I don't know how good of friends we are," Parker said.

Jeff edged nearer to Anita and looked into Parker's eyes. "That's harsh. Say what you will, but one thing is for sure, Anita is quickly becoming one hell of a *new* friend."

Parker imagined Jeff boiling in a huge stock pot in the kitchen. He could walk into the kitchen, grab a chef's knife, come back into the dining room, and jam it into Jeff's chest twisting his heart to shreds; then, drag him into the kitchen, quarter him, chop him, prepare a stock, throw him into a pot, cover the lid, boil, then simmer him until tender…just a thought.

"How 'bout if I make us all a little something to eat?" Parker said.

"That would be great," Jeff said moving even closer to Anita. "I could use a bite. Mind if we have a little more wine?"

"Drink up, my friend," Parker said.

Parker went into the kitchen, filled a small a pot of water, and placed it on a lit burner. He had some cooked pasta he could warm up once the water boiled. While waiting, he pulled a container beef stock and some braised pork from the refrigerator and simmered them together in a sauté pan. He threw in some fresh rosemary and a couple of sprinkles of red pepper flakes. He warmed a baguette in the oven and thought about his biggest stock pot while plating the three pasta dishes.

Parker returned to the dining room and noticed Jeff had opened another bottle of wine. Parker placed a bowl of pasta before each of them and sprinkled a little parmesan cheese on each dish. He placed the baguette in the center of the table.

"I hope you don't mind. The Amarone is excellent," Jeff said.

"Not at all," Parker said.

Jeff attacked his pasta greedily and swallowed the wine in enormous gulps. When eating, Jeff lost all of his poise and charm, leaning hunched over his plate, elbows on the table, and shoveling in large forkfuls of pasta. It was as if he reverted back to some primal survivalist. Anita and Parker watched him with curious amazement. When he finished, he pushed his plate forward, leaned back in his chair, and wiped his mouth with his napkin.

"You're a good cook, Parker," he said.

Anita continued to eat slowly and Parker had lost his appetite.

"I don't know how you missed the boat," Jeff said. "I mean you make great food and you don't get any recognition. I don't read about you in the paper. You're never on any of the best restaurant lists or top chef lists. It's like nobody knows you're around. How's business… you doing okay here?"

"I get by pretty well," Parker said.

"Well, it's a damn shame," Jeff said.

"Every night I've worked here we've been busy. This restaurant gets its business through word of mouth. People talk and recommend it to one another. That's better than any phony list," Anita said.

"It's still a damn shame. Publicity is good to have," Jeff said.

Parker was uncomfortable joining in on this conversation. Jeff's comments hit a raw nerve. His lack of recognition in the local paper and amongst other local chefs played heavily on his esteem. Knowing some of these hacks were basking in the glory of positive publicity brought Parker to depressive lows.

"I guess some of us hit our marks, and some of us

don't," Jeff said placing his hand on Anita's shoulder and looking at Parker with a wry smile. "Do you mind if I use your restroom?"

"Sure, why don't you use the one in the kitchen," Parker said. "Come on, I'll show you where it is."

They walked through the kitchen and Parker pointed to a small room with a toilet and a sink off to the side. Jeff stood in front of the toilet, unzipped his pants and pissed while Parker reached for his extra-large heavy-duty meat tenderizer mallet. The one with the wooded handle and dual-sided spiked-face hammer head.

"Yeah, it's too bad," Jeff said, shaking his pecker and finishing his piss. "You're losing out by not having any publicity. A restaurant needs publicity."

Parker raised the mallet and brought it down hard on the back of Jeff's head. Jeff's skull collapsed with a dull thump. His knees sagged to the floor and Parker pushed his head into the toilet and pressed it into the yellowed water until Jeff convulsed no longer. Parker dragged Jeff into a walk-in cooler and locked the door with a padlock. He took down the large stockpot off of a shelf and placed it on the stove. He glanced at a rack holding various knives and cleavers, and walked carefully back into the dining room. Anita greeted him with warm dark eyes.

"Jeff got a call on his cell phone and left," Parker

said. "He said somebody needed something and he needed to get to him right away. He apologized and bolted out the backdoor."

Anita nudged closer to Parker.

"Well, quite honestly, he really wasn't adding much to our evening," she said, with a warm smile.

"No," Parker agreed. "He really wasn't."

ALL OF tHe POSSibiLitieS

Judy sat slouched at her kitchen table. She stirred milk and three spoonsful of sugar into a large mug of coffee. She had a pounding headache. Max was still asleep, passed out cold from last night. Judy pieced together the evening, the arguments, the beer and the whiskey. Judy was thinking she didn't need to put up with Max anymore. *He was rotten, she thought. He really was.*

Max wandered from the bedroom to the bathroom. He rinsed his mouth with Listerine and looked into the mirror. His face was dull, his eyes two cloudy slits. He felt slightly nauseous and dizzy. He moved naked into the kitchen. It was a bright day outside. The sun tried to enter through the filthy grime that clung to the windowpanes leaving the room a dull piss color.

"What time is it?" Max asked.

"It's past noon," Judy answered.

"Why didn't you wake me up?"

"Why should I?"

"Don't start with me," he said. "You know I have to

work with Danny painting that house. He wants me there a hell of a lot earlier than now."

Max opened the door to the refrigerator, pulled out a carton of orange juice, and drank from it.

"You're nasty," Judy said.

"What?"

"The things you say."

"Don't start on me," Max said. "I was drunk."

"You're *always* drunk."

"I was drunker than usual and so were you."

"The things you say, Max. Calling me a whore and a bitch."

"I don't remember calling you those things."

"You did. Plenty of times."

*****

The evening started off promising. They ordered from the drive-through at the new Popeye's Louisiana Kitchen on Elmwood Avenue and grabbed an eight piece chicken dinner with coleslaw, Cajun fries, and biscuits. Max brought a bottle of whiskey, a liter of club soda, and a backpack cooler filled with ice. It was a bright and peaceful evening. They sat on a grassy embankment in Delaware Park looking over Hoyt Lake, eating, and slugging back whiskey and sodas. Joggers, dog walkers, and families with little kids strolled past. After finishing the chicken, Max threw the bones into the lake and a woman walking past gave him a haughty look.

"Fuck her," Max said, turning to Judy, while watching the woman move away from him.

"You should have thrown those in a garbage can, Max," Judy said. "There's some lined up by that restaurant over there."

"Fuck you, too," Max said, and made two more whiskey and sodas.

"You're impossible," Judy said.

"I'm sorry. Come here and give me a kiss," he said, pressing his mouth onto hers and placing his hand between her legs.

"Give me a smoke," Judy said, pushing away from him. "Let's have a smoke."

Max pulled two Marlboros from the pack in his shirt pocket, lit them both, and handed one to Judy. They sat silently smoking and drinking their whiskey and sodas. When they finished, they flicked their cigarettes into the lake and Max announced that it was time to leave.

They ended up at Kelly's Korner on Delaware Avenue. The regular crew was inside the dark bar looking like they'd been drinking for days. Tommy and Linda, Rich and Becky, and Timmy with his dimwitted brother Wally stood around a table filled with empty shot glasses and bottles of Labatt's Blue. That's where Max really started to hit the whiskey hard. He ordered double whiskey and sodas followed by shots of Jack. Judy drank her whiskey and sodas right along with Max, feeling that life was one dirty trick and these people she was hanging with were good for nothing. The more Wally drank the more he stared at Judy's ass. She watched him stupidly sneak looks and she was just done with it all, except she really did not know how to stop.

Max suggested the group play darts.

"Boys against the girls," he said. "Wally, you just keep getting us drinks when we need 'em."

"Sure thing, Max," Wally said. "You want a drink now, Max?"

"Fuck yes...shot of Jack, my friend," Max said.

The trouble started when the game was tied and Judy tossed a bulls-eye. It was her turn and when the dart bolted into the center of the board the girls screamed and high-fived one another.

"Lucky shot," Max muttered.

"Oh, I don't know," Judy teased, "I got some skills."

"Yeah, being a bitch and a whore," Max said.

"The hell with you," Judy answered.

"Oh, don't be such a little fuck, Max," Linda said.

"Yeah," Becky said. "We beat you fair and square."

"Fuck all of you bitches," Max said.

"All of you bitches," Wally repeated.

"Alright," Tommy said. "It's a fucking dart game. Everybody lighten up."

Rich suggested everyone have another beer and relax. He looked at Max and said, "This is supposed to be fun you stupid prick. Relax!"

Judy drove home. Max was passed out in the front seat, his head pressed awkwardly against the window. Bastard. *He'll probably have a stiff neck in the morning, Judy thought. Good.*

When they got to their apartment Max headed to the bedroom, took off his clothes, and climbed into bed. Judy took her clothes off and went into the bathroom. She washed her hands and face and brushed her teeth. When she got in bed Max moved on top of her. They moved about awkwardly until settling into a rhythm with Max pounding furiously until Judy let out a long, hard cry as she climaxed. He was asleep moments later.

Well, at least he's good at that, she thought, listening to him snore in the darkness.

*****

After Max went to work Judy contemplated what

to do. She enjoyed having time to herself. It was Saturday and she did not have to be at the salon until Monday. She took pleasure in the much needed break from breathing in harsh hair chemicals, standing nine hours a day over scalp after scalp, brushing, cutting, washing, rinsing, and listening to all of that draining babble from old ladies. It took a toll on her. She put in her time, though. It took her three years to get that schedule, having the weekends off.

When the phone rang, Judy figured it was probably her mother.

"Hello?"

"How are you, sweetheart?"

"I'm good, Mom…what's going on?"

"Oh, you know, not too much," Judy's mother said. "I'm trying to get your father to take me to the nursery. They have a sale on impatiens and I want to put some around that big tree in the backyard. I think they'll really brighten up the yard; but he's being *impossible* and doesn't want to go."

Judy warmed her coffee, lit a cigarette, took an ashtray from the kitchen table, and moved onto the front porch. She sat in a worn wicker chair and placed her feet on a wicker stool before her. Her mother continued.

"I want to get up and *do* something, but your father shows no interest in helping out with the yard. Does he think it's just going to happen by itself?"

"Probably not," Judy said.

"Well, it won't so he's going to *have* to pitch in and help me," Judy's mother said. "So, what did you do last night?"

"Not much," Judy said. "We had a little picnic at Delaware Park and then met up with some friends."

"So, you went out with *him*?" Judy's mother said.

"Of course I went out with *him*; we went out *together*," Judy said.

"You know your father is not very fond of him, says there's something off about that boy and your father does not like it one bit. I have to agree with him, baby. There's just something about him that doesn't click."

Judy took one more long pull from her cigarette and butted it into the ashtray. Listening to her mother talk about Max frustrated her, but she knew she was right. She was just looking out for her like she always did.

"He's okay," Judy said.

"Your father doesn't seem to think he's very nice to you. And what kind of future does he have painting houses? Honey, you can come home anytime, right back here to your room. Your father wants to turn your room into a TV room with one of those big flat screen TV's, but I'm not going to let that happen, that's your room and it's going to stay your room. Besides, he doesn't need to watch all that TV. It's all junk, anyway."

"I'm fine, Mom," Judy said.

"Well, your father says he's not nice and I can agree with that. Any time, baby…anytime you're ready, you come home."

"Okay, Mom," Judy said.

They hung up. Judy went into the kitchen, grabbed another cigarette and lit it. Dull smoke swirled into the heavy air. She mixed herself vodka with soda and moved back to the porch. It was sunny and warm. A gentle fragrant breeze let the leaves on the oak and elm trees dance delicately before her. Judy contemplated her mother's offer. Why *not* move back? It *would* be comfortable. Her parents were easy enough to get along with. She could move back and complete her Communications degree, do something she really wanted to do like work at a TV station or a radio station or something like that. She liked the stuff she was studying before she met Max. Before he held his grip on her.

The vodka and soda went down easy. Judy felt the slow syrupy warmth flow through her, loosening her. She decided to mix another drink. She felt relaxed. She spent the afternoon smoking cigarettes, drinking tall iced vodka and sodas, and watching the sun arc brilliantly across a row of houses on the other side of the street.

She remembered a time when she was a little girl and her mother and father took her on a road trip to Maine. They had driven through the night and Judy slept most of the way in the back seat. The next day they hiked along the rugged Bold Coast. They hiked through meadows and forests of spruce and fir trees at one point perching themselves atop a giant rocky cliff and watching the wild foamy surf pounding below. The coast stretched for miles with no signs of civilization anywhere. Seagulls zigzagged haphazardly above and seals lounged along the craggy shoreline. Beyond them lay the black-grey wide open sea, her waves rolling violently toward the shore. They watched silently.

"All the possibilities of life lie beyond the openness of the sea, Judy," her father said, wrapping his arm around her shoulders. "Look closely, it's there for the taking my little one."

Judy remembered that day well, remembered the closeness she shared with her parents and the comfort of that trip. She lit another cigarette and waited for Max, knowing he would be home soon. She would switch to whiskey and soda when he arrived.

A Funeral For Two:
A Memoir

As I recall it...

Friday, 11 May 2014: Maria and I landed in West Palm Beach on a bright sunny morning, picked up our tiny bright red Mazda rental car, stopped into Publix and bought a pineapple, bananas, almonds, and a twelve pack of Tecate beer. Then, we headed to the liquor store just down the street, grabbed a bottle of dark Meyer's Rum, and drove over the high-arched Blue Heron Bridge to Sunshine Shores apartments on Singer Island where my Dad and his wife Debbie had lived for a few years.

Sunshine Shores is *old school* Florida...two stories of white-washed concrete apartments with white wrought iron fences surrounds a clear blue pool and courtyard filled with palms, wisterias, and tropical plants. The owner of the place, Derek (a transplant from Brooklyn with a thick accent and a flat lid Yankee's cap), gave us our keys and we quickly went into our room, changed into our bathing suits, packed a cooler with beer, and headed to the pool. It was hot and bright and the water was soft blue and warm. We claimed a couple of vacant lounge chairs poolside. A few people from Canada and Boston and a slender guy with a soft lyrical voice named Wayne who *lost it all* after a relationship went sour waded in the pool clutching cans of Bud Light. Wayne was living with his brother, a construction worker, in my dad's old apartment.

My dad's apartment was at the end of a walkway that led from the pool to his front door. He had lived there with his wife Debbie, a tough, determined woman twenty-five years younger than him, for a couple of years. They previously lived in Redington Beach on the other coast for about twenty years until Debbie came down with a cancer that exploded from her brain forcing them to sell their house, and just about everything else of value, to help pay for the tremendous medical bills they had so quickly acquired.

Blind, immobile, and silent, Debbie withered and wilted toward death, as my dad tended to her bedside, wiping her brow and holding her hand until, on a hot rainy evening, she expired surrounded by her mother, brothers and sisters and my dad. As a last gesture, my dad coated her lips with a bit of Jameson Irish Whiskey and prayed for her soul's eternal peace and happiness.

The last couple of years of my dad's life were spent sitting poolside, smoking Cohiba cigars, reading newspapers, and hitting the local happy hours at Johnny Longboats and the Tiki Bar at the pink hotel across the street with an old construction manager from Montreal they called Frenchy. He spent evenings sipping Cuban rum, watching television shows and reading scripture, presumably trying to understand the mysteries and purpose of life and loss. The readings helped him to connect with his wife, whose ashes rested in a cherry-wood box on a table next to his bed.

My brother Kevin arrived in the early afternoon. His room was two doors down from ours. He lounged with us at the pool for a bit, drinking a couple of the iced Tecate's, and then headed to the airport to pick up his wife, Sharon, who was flying in from Denver. They arrived back at the pool about an hour later. We were still drinking the iced Tecates. The four of us relaxed under a beaming sun for a bit, then went back to our rooms and got dressed for dinner.

We had dinner at a place called Kee Grill. Like most of the restaurants I've been to in Florida, the food was fair, predictable, and over-priced. A waiter offered us a huge menu of Seafood, steaks, chicken…that kind of stuff. The place reminded me of an upscale Denny's nestled in a shopping plaza. In Florida, they're mostly all in a shopping plaza. It was crowded though and we had a decent dinner with drinks and wine. The bill was over four-hundred bucks.

After dinner we went to Johnny Longboats on Singer Island and drank bottles of Imperial beer in the loud, crowded bar while waiting for Debbie's sister Darlene and her husband, Journee, to arrive from Tampa.

Johnny Longboat's is always busy. A jam-packed and enormous oval bar takes up the center of the restaurant. Locals and tourists sit under giant overhead hangings of sharks and crabs and every other nautical ornament you can imagine. Surrounding the bar are clusters of tables filled with loud, tanned and sunburned diners digging into giant plates of fried and broiled seafood. We knocked back a bunch of those Imperials and waited quite a while until finally Darlene texted me and said she was across the street at a place called Buddy's.

Buddy's is a bar on Singer Island that gets a bad rap as a place where trouble happens on a nightly basis. We walked in and the place was crowded and smoky. A band on stage belted out Pearl Jam songs. It took me a minute to focus. At the end of the bar a slender woman with chestnut blonde hair, a tight fitted white dress and clear sunglasses sat with her legs crossed, smoking a cigarette. Next to her sat a brunette who I did not pay much attention to. I walked to the blonde and asked, "Are you Darlene?" and she gave me a vacant look and I realized *she* was Journee and the brunette was Darlene.

We all hugged and introduced ourselves and Kevin ordered a round of Guinness. We drank the creamy beer and followed that up with another round alongside shots of Jameson and Baileys and watched this loud band belting out the tunes. We all agreed to meet for breakfast the next morning at a place called Two Drunken Goats. Darlene said she and Journee had better leave now because if we were going to meet for breakfast, Journee would need to get to sleep. She would have to get up at four in the morning because it takes her four hours to put her make-up on.

At this point, my brother, Sharon, Maria and I were feeling warm and loose. We decided to go back to Sunshine Shores, grab a few beers, and head to the beach. We got our stuff and headed across the street, stumbling in a thick wooded area before finding a clearing and making it to the beach. It was very windy and we jumped into the warm Atlantic. A deep black sky was loaded with brilliant bright stars and brash waves pounded the shore knocking Sharon from side to side like a rag-doll.

Afterwards, we headed back and jumped into the

pool. The water was warm and the air was steamy. We waded in the water finishing our beers and then went back to our rooms. I think it only took a minute for me to fall asleep.

Saturday, 12 May 2014: The next morning I woke with a dry mouth and a pounding headache. The four of us headed to Two Drunken Goats, a restaurant with a big outdoor patio and a huge circular bar inside. The Goats has a breakfast special that includes Bloody Marys or screwdrivers for two bucks a piece...limit two. We ordered the Bloody Marys with eggs and hash browns and let the food settle in our stomachs. My head felt dull and cloudy from the night before. A couple of my dad's buddies were at the bar and they sent us over a shot of Fireball for each of us saying, "These are on Chuck!" That was the last thing I needed, but I knocked it back anyway.

For most of the afternoon we had a bunch of errands to run. Sharon took off and had to go back to Denver. Our hangovers eased. I don't remember all of the details of that afternoon, but I remember going to the marina to make sure we were set for the funeral the next day. The boat was ready and the captain and his crew were hired. I remember later in the evening Maria and my brother Kevin and I went to Johnny Longboats and met up with the rest of Debbie's family: her mother Hermi, brother Robert, two nephews (Jack-Michael and Douglas), sister Donna and husband Rex, and Darlene and Journee. They were sitting at a big table and we joined them after we had our dinner at the bar.

Sunday, 13 May 2014: That morning everyone arrived at our room and we joined my dad's ashes with Debbie's ashes, putting them in yellow cheese cloth and placing them in an ornate aqua-shelled box that Maria had purchased back in Buffalo. Debbie's sister Donna brought along a dozen long stemmed roses. Maria made a fine arrangement, placed it on a table, and we all took pictures.

Next, it was time to go to the marina for the ceremony. We brought the box down from our room and placed it in the back seat. My brother put the seatbelt around it announcing, "Safety first!"

Upon arriving at the marina others joined us. They had been invited by my father previously as he had planned his funeral down to every detail. We were greeted by a slightly built Irishman wearing red shoes, red socks, red pants, and a red button down shirt. He had a thick head of wiry gray hair and a kind face. He was going to take some of my dad's and Debbie's ashes and scatter them in Ireland. We divvied up some of the ashes and gave him his share. Along with the Irishman were a young couple and their daughter, friends my dad and Debbie knew for years. There was another man who brought along his loud boisterous son who laughed often and wore a baseball hat with a tarpon across it, and there was Sandra, Robert's friend, who wore a long floral sun dress with dark sunglasses covering her eyes.

The woman who ran the marina had us sign some paperwork and directed us to the boat. Our procession strolled down a long dock and onto a wide-bowed boat moored before us. Our stomachs felt hollow as they do when approaching funerals or when death is present, but there was also levity…a sense of celebration as my father had planned all of the details of his funeral. He had explained this to me on many occasions. In the final years of his life and especially after Debbie had died, he spoke of his funeral often, letting me know every detail to carry out. He wanted us to be sure we had Havana Club Rum and Kalik beer, we did. Dad instructed us to play Bob Marley music and we had to play *Let's Get Drunk and Screw,* by Jimmy Buffet.

My wife, Maria, carried the box aboard and we placed it on a bench near center aft. The Captain and his two mates greeted us and gave us a few brief instructions.

"The life preservers are here…when we get out about a mile and a half, we can begin the ceremony… it's going to be rough out there, the waves are high, hang tight if you need to."

Once we were all aboard, we assembled aft for a group photo. I believe the Captain took the photo. We motored slowly out from the dock and through the waterways leading to the ocean. We drank the beer and the slow easy beats of Bob Marley wafted from the speakers. We took pictures of the magnificent houses along the way, one more luxurious than the next. "Wouldn't that be a great one to live in…I'll bet they go for five million, at least." We cruised slowly through that little patch of waterway that separates Singer Island from West Palm Beach and we entered the ocean. The waves and swills were fairly high and the boat rocked and tossed about relentlessly. We needed to pay attention to balancing ourselves and develop our sea-legs on the spot. My brother Kevin was feeling the nausea of seasickness and found a bench under the bridge to lie on and try to regain composure. It never happened; he stayed in that position moaning and twisting until we returned to shore.

I believe we had to be about a mile out or so until we could begin the service. The Captain steered the boat to the desired nautical landing and he shut down the engines and all of us, except Keven, assembled aft and began the service.

I had made a brochure and selected some prayers so we could have at least some semblance of a formal send off. On the cover was a picture of my dad and Debbie. They were sitting at a beach café; my dad was holding a menu looking at the camera. Debbie was sitting closely with her arm around him; she was smiling into the camera. A warm sunlight illuminated them.

I believe the first reading was done by Jack-Michael, Debbie's nephew. He read from *Song of Solomon 2:10-13*, a beautiful piece that pays homage to a love between a husband and wife. Next, Douglas, another nephew, read *The Twenty-Third Psalm*. The words were moving and we listened closely as we rocked unsteadily on the Atlantic. Debbie's brother gave a moving reading of *Death is Nothing at All* by Henry Scott-Holland. Debbie's mother read a beautiful Buddhist saying: *When you are born, you cry, and the world rejoices. When you die, you rejoice, and the world cries.* She read it slowly and beautifully with tears filling her eyes. I read the Irish Blessing: *May the roads rise up to meet you...* and then it was time to inter my dad and Debbie into the Atlantic Ocean, in a current that would supposedly stream them toward Ireland…as they wished and believed in.

Darlene and I gently pulled their ashes from the aqua-shelled box, wrapped in the yellow cheese cloth, cradling it together in our hands. The boat bounced and tossed against the waves and it was difficult to stay balanced. Kevin remained on the bench puking in a bucket. Darlene and I inched closer to the small wooden deck above the engine planting our feet firmly and watching one another so that we would toss them in gently with one graceful swooping motion. Everyone had a handful of rose petals that Donna had brought and passed to each of us and Maria began a slow version of *Amazing Grace* on a wooden recorder that Debbie had given her a couple of years earlier. I gave Darlene a nod and we gently tossed the wrapped ashes in one steady motion low and into the water.

The bag sank and disappeared. The only sound was the long, soft notes from the recorder. Everyone threw a handful of rose petals into the water and there was nothing to see but the swirl of the Atlantic. They were gone. It felt anti-climactic, the ashes just sank, disappeared, until a moment later when a bright, fluorescent, translucent, aqua-blue stream rose to the surface and joined the floating rose petals stretching before us. Everyone peered out into the ocean and took in this enchanted sight, tears streaming from some. The luminous stream stretched further and further until all had blended into the ocean and disappeared. We bounced amongst the waves watching the rose petals growing smaller and smaller in the distance, and then we turned up Bob Marley and each took a nip of Havana Club Rum and toasted the lives and love story of my dad and Debbie.

Acknowledgements

My sincerest thanks to Brenden, Tara, Emily, and Quinn for your endless devotion and continuous inspiration. Thank you Quinn Haggerty for your help creating the cover for this book. Thank you Sarah Page for editing these stories and for your brutally honest advice that have made these stories publishable. Thank you Mark Pogodzinski and NFB Publishing for your patience and help with the design and layout and all of those other details that go along with publishing a book. And thank you Buffalo and Western New York for your strength, your people, and boundless inspiration for storytelling.

www.ingramcontent.com/pod-product-compliance
Lightning Source LLC
Chambersburg PA
CBHW021220250626
47155CB00008B/2899